Contemporary Chinese Poetry
in English Translation Series

Xi Chuan
Selected Poems

Translated by Lucas Klein, Maghiel van Crevel
and others

教育部人文社会科学重点研究基地
安徽师范大学中国诗学研究中心 组编
Chinese Poetry Research Center of Anhui Normal University

杨四平 主编　　上海文化出版社

当代汉诗英译丛书

西川诗歌英译选

CONTENTS

Part 1

目录

卷一

Part 2

卷二

Part 1

卷一

DEAD PANTHER

Pale brown panther
its tale quietly taps the moss on
the rock, taps
my palm

It moves, like a garden would move
pearls of wild grapes
roll in the wind, and the bashful
thyme radiates pale rays of light

No flesh is moving
We cannot call flesh
this old panther, softly drifting
indolent water, relaxed and vigilant

I hear the cold sound of water in my palm
It exudes from its feet sole to my palm
the sound of water surges from heeling bloody sky
and in its eyes some serenity

死豹

棕黄色的豹子
尾巴敲打着落满青苔的
山岩，敲打着
我的手掌

它移动，像一座花园在移动
野生的葡萄珠
在风中滚动，而羞涩的
百里香射出苍白的光芒

没有运动的肉体
我们不能称之为肉体
这只年迈的豹子，轻柔地飘移
流水般疏懒，放松警惕

我听到水的泠泠声在我的手掌上
从它的脚下渗出在我的手掌上
水声激荡结疤的红霞
而它的眼睛里一片安详

Now, it wants to control the way it will die

yield to the garden on its back

firmly grabbing a little dirt from the splendid flowers

its tales taps the rock

taps my green palm as if it were an angel's palm

ah flower, ah water, the rock falls backward

an unreal image appears

it peacefully sleeps on my green palm

Thus I get a piece of amber hanging down my waist

And it's earth's treasure

Translated by Sarah Anais Aubry

现在，它要按自己的方式死去
让背上的花园
攫住一寸泥土开出绚烂的花
它的尾巴敲打山岩

敲打我大天使绿色的手掌
花呀水呀，山岩退后
幻影出现
它在我绿色的手掌上安眠

从此我据有一块琥珀垂挂腰间
而它本是大地的宝藏

1986.5

A BLACK BIRD

A blackbird cawing

a blackbird spreading its wings in shadow

a sheet of black paper, a blackbird climbing

flying up on a current of air

crosses over city walls in winter

over a forest of few trees, frozen smoke

A deep red man, all winter

hesitating at the end of the corridor

he dreamed of this blackbird

like a sound at dawn after snow

above time, above reason

growing beautiful, rich in hidden meaning

A cawing blackbird

is not the form found in our hidden feelings

it has the highest blue sky

it has no relation to this world

it is purely a mistaken impression

since the white snow burnt our eyes blind

Translated by Michael Day

黑鸟

一只呱呱叫着的黑鸟
一只在阴影中展开双翼的黑鸟
一片黑纸，一只攀着气流
向上飞去的黑鸟
越过冬季的城垣
越过荒疏的林带、冻结的烟

深红色的男人，整个冬天
在走廊的尽头徘徊
他梦见过这只黑鸟
像雪后黎明的一种声音
在时间之上，在理性之上
变得美丽，富于暗示

一只呱呱叫着的黑鸟
不是我们的隐衷所找到的形象
它有无上的青天
它与这世界无关
它是纯粹的一个错觉
因为白雪烧瞎了我们的双眼

1988.10

In SEARCH OF THE SEA

In a place where mountain ridges loom
I search for the sea
I look for a pirate who signals with a lamp
look for an organism called a seahorse
kiss a hexagon of flo-ice

I look for mountain ridges on that sea
the green of a stern trees loved passionately by you
a sun that passes through my chest
disturbs the sandy soil over the tree roots
I look for gold ore in that sandy soil

What I look for is a promise
horses on the stones, you sing so well
the sound of your song stops at ocean bottom of those deserted streets
those houses, I remember them
the instruments out of sequence, I like cards, can't foretell the future

I hear seawater
hear the power of a dark blue love in the latter half of the night
if I were a rock
what would the water flowing through my heart be
and who is it that pins the flowers of ocean stones to a dark overcoat

寻找海洋

在山脊高耸的地方
我寻找海洋
我寻找一名制作灯语的海盗
寻找一种叫做海马的生物
吻过的六角浮水

我寻找山脊在那海洋上
船头的绿色你们热爱过的树木
从我胸中穿过的太阳
搬动树根上的沙土
我寻找的是那沙土中的黄金

我寻找的是一个诺言
石头上的马儿你多会歌唱
你的歌声停在海底那些空荡荡的街道上
那些房屋我记住它们
那些失灵的仪器像纸牌算不出未来

我听见海水
听见藏青色的爱情在后半夜的威力
如果我是岩石
我心中的流水又是什么
又是什么人将海石花别在暗色的外套上

What sound will not change for a thousand years

like a storm at sea unabated for a thousand years

the mammoths wrestling by the riverside appear to lie down

and become coal as they sleep? Hey, you nonexistent miner

I want the miner's lamp you never had

Light the rugged way

the rough sea route

what I look for is a vast expanse of coral sea

in the mind's azure sea

a fisherman flashes into being the dark shape of my father's back

Translated by Michael Day

什么声音千年不化
像海洋上的风暴千年不息
角力的猛犸象在哪一条河流边安卧
睡成煤？呵，不存在的矿工
我要你不曾有过的矿灯

照着崎岖的道路
崎岖的航线
我寻找的是一片珊瑚汪洋
它蔚蓝色的脑海里
一个打渔人闪现我父亲的背影幽暗

1986.8

PREMONITION

I hang bright mirrors high on the wall
you let dark clouds in through the doorway

You bring a city beneath the clouds in through the doorway
and the city in the mirrors is plastered with slogans
you bring a village beneath the clouds in through the doorway
and the village in the mirrors burns with torches

Eagles in the mirrors, horses in the mirrors
soaked in a downpour, intimate with sufferings
my mirrors repel misery
but you lead a lion out of the gunfire

And then you lead the night out of thought
and wind from dejection
and you bring the wing through the doorway
where it buffets the mirrors: the mirrors of my forebears

预感

我把明镜高悬于四壁
你把乌云引进大门

你把乌云下的城市引进大门
镜中的城市贴满标语
你把乌云下的乡村引进大门
镜中的乡村闪耀着火炬

镜中的鹰、镜中的马
被大雨浇淋从而熟知苦难
我的明镜拒绝苦难
而你又从炮火中引来了狮子

你又从思想中引来了黑夜
你又从苦闷中引来了风
你把风引进大门
它敲着明镜：我祖先的明镜

Carrying the sighs of strangers
and I can hear the immortality of their spirits in these sighs
you bring the spirits in through the doorway
and I make up a low bed for them

For you, I make up a heap of rice straw
I want to capture you in the mirrors
to make you make up before you sleep
to make you bring sleep in through the doorway

No sleep, no sleeper
scissor, ink and tea bowls
the mirrors reflect the last meal
you bring dawn light through the doorway

Translated by John Keley

它带来陌生者的浩叹
我从这浩叹听出灵魂的不朽
你把灵魂引进大门
我为他们安排下歇脚的床铺

我也为你安排下稻草一堆
我要用明镜把你捉住
让你在睡眠前梳妆打扮
让你把睡眠引进大门

没有睡眠，没有睡眠的
剪刀、墨水和茶杯
明镜映照最后的晚餐
你把晨光引进大门

1991.7

TWELVE SWANS

The twelve swans shining on the lake
have no shadows

Those twelve swans reluctant to part from each other
are hard to approach

Twelve swans -- twelve musical instruments --
when they call

When they wield wings like silver
the air sustains their bulky
bodies

An era withdraws to one side, with its
Jibes

Think of it, twelve swans and me
live in the same city!

Those twelve swans shining on the lake
make flesh quiver hearts quake

Between water and ducks, they keep
a pure bestial nature

十二只天鹅

那闪耀于湖面的十二只天鹅
没有阴影

那相互依恋的十二只天鹅
难于接近

十二只天鹅——十二件乐器——
当它们鸣叫

当它们挥舞银子般的翅膀
空气将它们庞大的身躯
托举

一个时代退避一旁，连同它的
讥诮

想一想，我与十二只天鹅
生活在同一座城市！

那闪耀于湖面的十二只天鹅
使人肉跳心惊

在水鸭子中间，它们保持着
纯洁的兽性

Water is their acreage
froth is their jewelry

Once we dream of these twelve swans
their haughty necks
bend toward the water

What keeps them from sinking?
Is it the webbing of their feet?

Reliant on the physiognomy of feathers
they recover lost amulets time after time

Unlimited lake water, a distant high sky: poetry
Superfluous

I'd so like to see ninety-nine swans
born in the moonlight!

You must become a swan, before you can tail
along behind --
navigate by constellation

Or from the leaves of water hyacinth and lotus
suck up the black night

Translated by Michael Day

水是它们的田亩
泡沫是它们的宝石

一旦我们梦见那十二只天鹅
它们傲慢的颈项
便向水中弯曲

是什么使它们免于下沉?
是脚蹼吗?

凭着羽毛的占相
它们一次次找回丢失的护身符

湖水茫茫,天空高远:诗歌
是多余的

我多想看到九十九只天鹅
在月光里诞生!

必须化作一只天鹅,才能尾随在
它们身后 ——
靠星座导航

或者从荷花与水葫芦的叶子上
将黑夜吸吮

1992.2

BATS AT TWILIGHT

In Goya's drawings they bring an artist
nightmares. They flicker
about him whispering secret things
but never wake him.

Unspeakable pleasures appear on their
human faces. The bodies of these bird-like
creatures are black and wedded to the darkness
like seeds that will never blossom.

They are like fettered spirits,
blind, cruel, led by their wills.
Sometimes they hang upside down on branches
pitiful as dead leaves.

But in other stories, they hang in dark caves,
and emerge at dusk,
probing for food and giving birth and then
flickering out of existence.

They'll waylay a dream walker,
wresting the torch from his hands and snuffing it dead
or they'll put a prowling wolf to flight
then drop silent through a valley.

夕光中的蝙蝠

在戈雅的绘画里，它们给艺术家
带来了噩梦。它们上下翻飞
忽左忽右；它们窃窃私语
却从不把艺术家叫醒

说不出的快乐浮现在它们那
人类的面孔上。这些似鸟
而不是鸟的生物，浑身漆黑
与黑暗结合，似永不开花的种籽

似无望解脱的精灵
盲目，凶残，被意志引导
有时又倒挂在枝丫上
似片片枯叶，令人哀悯

而在其他故事里，它们在
潮湿的岩穴里栖身
太阳落山是它们出行的时刻
觅食，生育，然后无影无踪

它们会强拉一个梦游人入伙
它们会夺下他手中的火把将它熄灭
它们也会赶走一只入侵的狼
让它跌落山谷，无话可说

If a child can't fall asleep at night
it means a bat is near,
whispering his fate
and eluding the night watchman's tired eyes.

One bat, two bats, three bats, they are poor and homeless,
so how should they bring us wealth?
The changing moon has stripped away their feathers;
they are ugly and anonymous.

Their hard hearts leave me cold,
but one summer at dusk
as I passed my old home I saw the children playing
while bats swarmed above their heads.

Twilight spread shadows in the hutong
but the bats were clothed with gold.
They flinted beyond the gate with its peeling paint
silent as their own fates.

Among ancient things, a bat
is surely a reminder, and there in the hutong
where I grew up I paused for a long while
watching their leisurely flight.

Translated by Tony Barnstone & the author

在夜晚，如果有孩子迟迟不睡
那定是由于一只蝙蝠
躲过了守夜人酸疼的眼睛
来到附近，向他讲述命运

一只，两只，三只蝙蝠
没有财产，没有家园，怎能给人
带来福祉？月亮的盈亏褪尽了它们的
羽毛；它们是丑陋的，也是无名的

它们的铁石心肠从未使我动心
直到有一个夏季黄昏
我路过旧居时看到一群玩耍的孩子
看到更多的蝙蝠在他们头顶翻飞

夕光在胡同里布下了阴影
也为那些蝙蝠镀上了金衣
它们翻飞在那油漆剥落的街门外
对于命运却沉默不语

在古老的事物中，一只蝙蝠
正是一种怀念。它们闲暇的姿态
挽留了我，使我久久停留
在那片城区，在我长大的胡同里

1991.2

A TUNE ON A PIANO AT MIDNIGHT

Luckily I can feel, luckily I can listen
at midnight a tune on a piano resurrects a spirit
in shadows a person walks toward me
a person without body can not be stopped
but he has the ability to polish lights and implements
make me ashamed to see my dirty black hands

The ice of sleep makes cracking sounds
in a flash azaleas blaze into bloom across the land
a man approaches me, I'm too late to dodge away
just as I'm too late to avoid my own green spring
amid a piano tune at midnight, I lick
cracked lips, awake to the necessity of life

But a tune on a piano at midnight is like me
a happiness that can't be caught, why is it this long
whatever I seize, its nature alters?
As if just now I remember the many raucous song and dance scenes
but tonight's tune is not to be accompanied by anyone
it is mysterious, distressed, a soliloquy

午夜的钢琴曲

幸好我能感觉，幸好我能倾听
一支午夜的钢琴曲复活一种精神
一个人在阴影中朝我走近
一个没有身子的人不可能被阻挡
但他有本领擦亮灯盏和器具
令我羞愧地看到我双手污黑

睡眠之冰发出咔咔的断裂声
有一瞬间灼灼的杜鹃花开遍大地
一个人走近我，我来不及回避
就像我来不及回避我的青春
在午夜的钢琴曲中，我舔着
干裂的嘴唇，醒悟到生命的必然性

但一支午夜的钢琴曲犹如我
抓不住的幸福，为什么如此之久
我抓住什么，什么就变质？
我记忆犹新那许多喧闹的歌舞场景
而今夜的钢琴曲不为任何人伴奏
它神秘，忧伤，自言自语

Outside the window the strong wind stops, there must be a hawk
flying close to a snow-capped peak, there must be a peacock
aroused by an illusion, in the starlight extending a screen
and I'm like a sunflower standing at the center of midnight
asking myself who will take away my cumbersome life
a man approaches me, we seem to know each other

We stand face to face, identifying each other
I hear somebody far off applauding
a tune on a piano at midnight returns to silence
Right, it's like this: a man approaches me
hesitates a moment, an immediate urge to speak suppressed
turns back to the boundless shadow to which he belongs

Translated by Michael Day

窗外的大风息止了，必有一只鹰
飞近积雪的山峰，必有一只孔雀
受到梦幻的鼓动，在星光下开屏
而我像一株向日葵站在午夜的中央
自问谁将取走我笨重的生命
一个人走近我，我们似曾相识

我们脸对着脸，相互辨认
我听见有人在远方鼓掌
一支午夜的钢琴曲归于寂静
对了，是这样：一个人走近我
犹豫了片刻，随即欲言又止地
退回到他所从属的无边的阴影

1994.1

SONG OF UNIMPORTANCE

It's not important whether a fly's called "fly."
Not important if its buzz gets louder and louder.
Not important if it drinks up ink and pisses blue
Not important if it decides to be excellent.

We two keep silent.

It's not important if the fly buzzes off and someone else enters the room.
Not important if he chatters away, happy and content,
clever enough, he says, to even have his way in heaven. When he leaves,
it's not important if he's the wisest man in paradise

We two keep silent.

Silence encloses not only us
but the power pole and its shadow afloat beyond the window.
It's not important if a kite hangs dead from the wires,
not important that around the pole we run thousands of miles.

Translated by Diana Shi & George O'Connell

无关紧要之歌

苍蝇叫不叫"苍蝇"无关紧要
它的嗡嗡声越来越大无关紧要
它喝了一肚子墨水撒出的尿全是蓝的无关紧要
它决定作一只优秀的苍蝇无关紧要

我们两人鸦雀无声

苍蝇飞走，房间里多了一个人无关紧要
他谈笑风生自得其乐无关紧要
他说他的聪明足以在天上吃得开，然后就走了
他是否成了天上最聪明的人无关紧要

我们两人鸦雀无声

鸦雀无声的还不仅只我们两人
还有窗外的电线杆和它移动的影子
电线杆上吊死一只风筝无关紧要
我们绕着电线杆跑了十万八千里无关紧要

2000.6

CORNERING SONG

I corner a raven against the wall
I want it to teach me the secret of flight
It sings "Spare me, sir" while it takes off its wings
Then it wrenches itself from me, spreads its little claws and flees to the
worldly path

I corner an old man against the wall
I want him to admit that I am even older
He takes out his wallet and begs "Spare me, sir!"
I hesitate just a moment, he tugs off my gold necklace, turns and runs
away

I corner a girl against the wall
I want her to praise the world for its grace
She loosens her buttons, trembling, says "Spare me, sir!"
Then she turns herself into a 200-watt bulb to light me up

I corner a black bear against the wall
I want it to eat me in a single gulp
It opens its blood-red mouth, says "Spare me, sir!"
I kill it with a single slap, and eat it in the moonlight

Translated by Luby Chow & Robert Neather

墙角之歌

我把一只乌鸦逼到墙角
我要它教给我飞行的诀窍
它唱着"大爷饶命"同时卸下翅膀
然后挣脱我，撒开细爪子奔向世俗的大道

我把一个老头逼到墙角
我要他承认我比他还老
他掏出钱包央求"大爷饶命！"
我稍一犹豫，他薅下我的金项链转身就逃

我把一个姑娘逼到墙角
我要她赞美这世界的美好
她哆嗦着解开扣子说"大爷饶命！"
然后把自己变成一只 200 瓦的灯泡将我照耀

我把一头狗熊逼到墙角
我要它一口把我吃掉
它血口一张说"大爷饶命！"
我一掌打死它，并且就着月光把它吃掉

2002.6
2010.2

ONE AFTERNOON

Gold's going up, investors sorry they waited.

Diamonds too. Surely some see diamonds are just stones.

Libya's war endless, Europe clutching the tiger's tail. All so remote.

Bin Laden shot dead in Pakistan. Too bad the Seal pulling the trigger
won't be famous.

Many tangled in the stock market, including clever friends.

Checking the latest quotes on their cellphones, they chat and chortle
as if texting love notes. Here and not here, they're utterly devoted yet
distracted.

The afternoon's so pleasant it seems fake. Clumps of white clouds dream
they're adrift over Paris.

Shopping centers styled like Europe's hamlets, so foreigners feel at
home,
so children dabbling in water get used to global consumption, while the
parents toy with cameras.

A dozen streams in the fountain dance high and low, confirming their
happiness.

The central jet suddenly shoots ten meters, like a magician grandly
closing his performance.

下午

黄金涨价，让储藏黄金的打算推迟，后悔当年的抠门。
钻石也涨价 —— 而钻石，不过是石头的一种 —— 必有人如此感
悟。

利比亚战事没完没了，欧洲的干预骑虎难下，但那都在远方。
本·拉登被击毙在巴基斯坦。可惜开枪的海豹突击队员永远出不
了大名。

股市套住了许多人，包括我那些智慧的朋友们。
他们总在说笑时翻看手机中的股市行情，好像在发短信谈情说爱。
他们生活在此处同时又生活在别处，专心致志同时又心不在焉。

美好的下午，像假的。团团白云以为自己飘动在巴黎的上空。
购物中心建成欧洲小镇的模样，使老外有归家之感；
使戏水的孩子们习惯于世界性消费，而家长们全在玩照相机。

人造喷泉的数十根水柱忽高忽低，表明它们是快乐的；
中心水柱忽然喷出十米之高，带着魔术师表演成功的得意。

A girl struts out of a cafe, tossing her hair, donning sunglasses. How sunshine loves her.

The straps of her pink bra show on her shoulders, her flipflops slap at her soles, "pip-pap."

A middle-school girl walks with Japanese mini-steps, but soon she'll return to Chinese

--marry a chicken, live like a chicken; marry a dog, live like a dog.

A middle-aged man from a small town suddenly finds himself in the palace of the gods, but can't grasp the foreign ads.

Still, he enjoys Titanic's theme song: new products should now be in the market.

Roped into surrendering an afternoon by my wife and child,

I find a free chair in a streetside café.

The sun creeps west along its arc, falling faster soon enough.

Since the wife's off shopping, the child skating, I dial a friend's number.

His phone off lately, now it rings through. I thought he'd been arrested, but he picks up.

His life's alright, but his mother's lung cancer has entered her bones. He's serving out his last filial duties.

We arrange to meet in two weeks, about nothing important.

Translated by Diana Shi & George O'Connell

从咖啡店走出的女孩甩头发，戴上墨镜。阳光爱着她。
她胸罩的粉红色肩带露在肩膀上，拖鞋打着脚底板发出"嘁嘁"
声响。

而比她更小的女中学生走着日本女孩的小碎步，不过将来
她还是会走回中国人的步伐，嫁鸡随鸡嫁狗随狗。

来自小县城的中年男人仿佛一下掉进了洞天福地，看不懂外文广
告，
却仍能享受电影《泰坦尼克号》抒情的主题曲：又该有新产品上市。

我坐在咖啡店的露天散座上，被老婆孩子要求让出一个下午。
偏西的太阳还在走它的弧线，一会儿更会加快速度。

但老婆去购物了，孩子去滑冰了，我给朋友打电话，通了。
我先前数次电他他都关机。我以为他被抓了起来但这次他接了电
话。
他活得好好的，但他母亲肺癌转骨癌。他尽着最后的孝道。

我们约好过两周见个面，其实也没什么要紧的事情。

2011.6

VISITING BEI DAO IN BELOIT, SEP. 2002

A thousand tons of clouds

scatter over Beloit like the steppe-sweeping Mongol cavalry;

Ten tons out of the thousand

rain down on Beloit like Mongol cavalry,

sweeping, raiding, sparing no small town.

If you turn over a leaf, drowned insects will appear.

If you enter an empty house, you'll be greeted by drenched, trembling

ghosts.

A sedan pulls up at a car motel.

The smoking room's lingering odor won't dissipate even if you prop the

door open.

Does the stranger chain-smoke three packs a day? You can imagine

his gloominess and self-abandonment

but the locals are even more somber:

When half the shelves are empty downtown

they don't bother to smoke, what a tribute to the lone-flying spangled flag

in the parking lot.

访北岛于美国伊力诺伊州伯洛伊特小镇。2002 年 9 月

一千吨乌云
像大草原上散开的蒙古骑兵呼拉移过伯洛伊特上空

一千吨乌云分出十吨乌云
砸向伯洛伊特像蒙古骑兵搂草打兔子绝不放过哪怕衰败不堪的小镇

翻开落叶，是溺死的昆虫
走进空屋，会撞见湿漉漉的鬼魂颤抖个不停

小汽车抵达小旅馆
小旅馆的吸烟房间里烟味淤积不散即使打开屋门

这吸烟的过客一天要吸三包烟吗？其忧郁和破罐子破摔的程度可
以想见
而本地人忧郁更甚

眼见得镇子上的一半橱窗空空如也
却绝不动起吸烟的念头，
这真对得起停车场上寂寞飘扬的美国国旗

At a three-way junction in Beloit,

only two or three people mumble on the steps below the bank,

only one cleaves an eggplant in two

in a rented white room, believing that his cooking could get him some

friends.

After sundown, night.

After night, an inevitable autumn for an exile.

An autumn robs a tree of its leaves

but only one man feels a chill down his spine, cowers like an atom,

then covers the scattering pages on his desk

as if a wind travels beyond the skyline just to meet him.

Translated by Weijia Pan

这是三岔路口上的伯洛伊特
只有两三个人在银行的台阶上低声交谈

只有一个人在借来的白房子里
用菜刀剖开紫茄子，相信烧一手好菜就能交到朋友

黄昏过后是夜晚
夜晚过后是只能如此、只好如此的流亡者的秋天

秋天将树叶一把揪走
只有一个人为此而心寒，瑟缩为一个原子

并且伸手捂住他桌上的纸页
仿佛天际一阵大风越过了地平线来到面前

2002.9
2009.8

AT TRAKLHOUSE, SALZBURG, AUSTRIA, JULY 2009

Rain in the morning, rain at night,
falling on Trakl's courtyard, but I wasn't there.

There, a porch with pillars pockmarked with nails;
There, a stone well capped, gazing through the iron grate.

In solitude, even a sigh sounds like a shriek.
His sister, recalling him, covered her tender ears.

How could a young man bridle the blood in his veins?
He wrote such melancholy and engrossing poems, but he feared

being dragged through the dusky fields, disposed of
in a deep forest that a future bride stumbled through.

He died in 1914. Now, those who know him
can discuss him objectively, distantly.

特拉克尔故居，奥地利萨尔茨堡。2009 年 7 月

早上一场雨，晚上一场雨
雨落在特拉克尔的庭院时我不在那里

被铁钉钉入的石柱撑住一楼的走廊
走廊边的石台深井被盖上了铁箅子

寂静中仿佛听到等同于尖叫的叹息
回想哥哥的小妹只好捂住粉嫩的耳朵

少年人怎禁得住血浆喷射的摧毁
他写忧郁的诗、紧握事物的诗，害怕

被横拖过黄昏的原野，被丢弃在
一个将要做新娘的姑娘偶然穿过的密林

他死于 1914 年。到如今，知道他
并且谈论他的人已可以和他拉开距离

In Salzburg, he used only a black staircase
and a doorway in a locked-up courtyard.

His pedals left mulberry traces on the moss-topped wellhead
but there's no one living to litter from his spotless balcony.

The ghost of Trakl knows it: his neighbor
the great Mozart, gregarious, a thriving chocolatier;

but he, a powerless ghost, only stirs
a little wind sometimes in his courtyard.

He continues with the tricks he despises,
minor sorrow wrapped in minor joy, minor sorrow in major sorrow.

Three young men flash past the gate to his courtyard.
He follows after them, but still isn't the fourth.

Translated by Weijia Pan

在萨尔茨堡，他只使用过一座庭院中的
一道黑色的楼梯和一道现在上了锁的小门

他的花瓣在井台的青苔上睡出紫红
但无人从那二楼洁白的窗口向外扔东西

鬼魂特拉克尔知道：他伟大的
邻居莫扎特，大活人，糖球生意做得很好

而他一无所长即使在他成为鬼魂之后
他只会有时在庭院中旋起小风一阵

让他自己也会轻蔑的小动作他一做再做
小快乐中套着小难过，小难过中套着大难过

三个青年闪过他家庭院的大门口
他疾步跟上他们，但依然不是第四个

2009.7.4 萨尔茨堡

ODE TO SKIN

Pillow creases on skin. The tiny feet of insects have left their prints –
poisonous bloodspots medicinally sucked out.

Skin – my silent surface. This skin of mine has never experienced
frenzied torture so it dreams of frenzied torture and thus slips into history.
Then grows a silent crop: hairs without a sense of history.

Landscapes on skin. Maps with pins. A Nazi lampshade made of human
skin. English books bound from girls' breasts in Chaucer's time.

A leather sofa doesn't have the dead cow's soul. But each time I get up
from it I can't help mooing three times.

Consort Yang Yuhuan's skin touched flowers. Concubine Wang Zhaojun's
skin touched ice. I have never met these skins so can only talk about
them.

When I stare at my skin with its buried veins I also see your skin in a
cool summer but can't see your bones.

Shameless bones coated with graceful skin. What makes graceful skin
shameless as bones? Only cheeks get shy and embarrassed.

皮肤颂

枕头的褶皱压在皮肤上。小虫子的小爪子在皮肤上留下印迹。拔火罐从皮肤之下拔出血点。有毒的血点。

皮肤。我寂静的表层。我这不曾遭受过酷刑的皮肤，幻想着酷刑，就进入了历史，就长出了寂静的庄稼：我这了无历史感的汗毛。

山水画在皮肤上。地图刺在皮肤上。纳粹的人皮灯罩。乔叟时代英格兰的图书封皮用少女乳房的皮肤制成。

沙发，以牛皮为自己的皮肤，却不具有那死去动物的灵魂。每一次从牛皮沙发上站起，我总是忍不住牛鸣三声。

她的皮肤遇到了花朵：杨玉环。她的皮肤遇到了冰：王昭君。那些我永远无法遇到的皮肤，我只是说说而已。

但当我注目我潜伏着血管的皮肤，我也就看见了你清凉在夏季的皮肤。但我还想看见你的骨头。

无耻的骨头，裹着雅洁的皮肤，遇到什么样的皮肤它就会瞬间变得像骨头一样无耻？只有面颊懂得害羞和尴尬。

Skin lines under a magnifying glass. Skin's greyness in the wardrobe mirror. Pockmarks, blackheads, freckles, goose bumps. Skin only speaks to those who read fortunes.

My skin contains my sickness, happiness and my darkness, which can't be illuminated by any light.

I have seven perpetual gates and temporary wounds. Sore skin and dead skin without nerve tips, corpse-skin. It's said that ghosts wander without skins. It's said that aliens think with their skins.

You approach me with your skin, or my skin can feel yours shivering. I'm not sure whether you want to flay me and put my skin on a sheep or a wolf.

Translated by Pascale Petit & the author

放大镜下皮肤的纹理。穿衣镜中皮肤的灰暗。麻子、痦子、疣子、鸡皮疙瘩。皮肤只将命运表达给能够读懂命运的人。

我的皮肤内装着我的疾病、快乐和幽暗。我的幽暗是灯光不能照亮的。

永久的七窍。临时性伤口。疼的皮肤。藏起来的皮肤。长在里面的皮肤。失去神经末梢的皮肤。死人的皮肤。

据说鬼魂没有皮肤也东游西逛。

据说太空人用皮肤来思想。

你用皮肤向我靠近，或者我用皮肤感受你的颤抖。我说不准你是否想要揭下我的皮肤去披到狼或者羊的身上。

2006.6

I HIDE MY TAIL

I hide my tail, blending in with others who hide their tails.

I stoop down, thinking I can get closer to my shadow, but my shadow also stoops, as if about to flee.

Swallowing cold water to full-stomach can drown all true thoughts.

Walking, I spread forth my hands, yet I am not pleading for anything. But, oh, what would fall into my hands of its own accord?

Finger cut on scrap glass, no mosquito is seen coming.

I train my eyes, making them as sharp as eagles' eyes. Finally I can see everything clearly, and the helplessness in my heart is inescapable.

If you come too close, I have no use for my binoculars. They are specially for seeing you, you should just stay in the distance.

Petals on the street – are they the beauty Xi Shi's broken nails?

If others do again the stupid thing I did, I can't stop them. If I do it once again myself, it's just that I want to show my trickiness.

我藏着我的尾巴

我藏着我的尾巴，混迹于其他藏着尾巴的人们中间。

我俯下身来，以为会接近我的影子，但我的影子也俯下身来，摆出一副要逃跑的姿势。

喝一肚子凉水就能淹死全部的心里话。

走着，我摊开手，但我不祈求世间任何东西。但是，啊，有什么东西会自动落入我的掌心？

碎玻璃割破手指，不见蚊子飞来。

我练习双眼，练得像鹰眼一样锐利。终于可以看清一切，内心的无奈便无法逃避。

如果你走得太近，我就用不上望远镜了。我的望远镜专为看你而准备，你应该仅仅待在远方。

街上的花瓣，是否西施的碎指甲？

我干过的蠢事别人再干，我无法阻止。我自己再干一遍，只是想显示我诡计多端。

I can't stand with madmen and look on helplessly when ordinary people do evil things, but
I can't stand with ordinary people and look on helplessly when madmen do evil things either.

A wise man would use up a whole day's sense by nightfall.

Raising my head to look at the moon, I keep ringing my bicycle bell, yet at the same time, I can't help but snort like a horse to the moon. On the moon, it is so peaceful.

It's Tuesday, a plume of smoke rises up from a blown-out candle.

It's Wednesday, flies from the south defeat those from the north.

With car exhaust fumes I entertain the gathering mice. They are glad and satisfied, and all agree: screw the world, but don't screw them up.

Don't scare humans, go and scare humans who are not human, they need to be threatened, like they need to be flattered.
I use a coin to imprint a pattern on your skin.

You figure out the weight of the sky. Just for fun, fine. But if you mean it, I will have to choke you to death.

Wanderer of the night, let's not meet.

Translated by Luby Chow & Robert Neather

既不能站在疯子一边对常人之恶束手无策，也不能站在常人一边对疯子之恶束手无策。

聪明人赶在天黑以前用完一天的理智。

抬头望月，我猛按车铃，同时忍不住像马一样朝月亮喷出响鼻。月亮上真安静。

星期二，吹熄的蜡烛上一屡青烟。

星期三，南方的苍蝇打败了北方的苍蝇。

我用汽车尾气招待聚会的老鼠。它们心满意足，一致同意：世界真该死，而它们不该死。

别吓唬人，去吓唬不是人的人吧，他们需要被吓唬，就像他们需要被讨好。

我用硬币在你的皮肤上压出图案。

你计算天空的重量。玩一玩，行。你若认真，我就只好把你掐死。

夜晚的游荡者，我们避免相识。

2004.11

GHOSTS OF THE SIX DYNASTIES

In the Six Dynasties (AD 265 ~ 588) ghosts outnumbered people. The living dreamed of ghosts at night, and ran into ghosts by day. Ghosts don't avoid sunlight, like how rats don't avoid people. Life in the Six Dynasties was queer: Look at "The Annals of Darkness," it says that ghosts also grew body hair, armpit hair, and pubic hair. Ghosts vied with humans for food and fought amongst themselves.

The ghosts of the Six Dynasties were well educated. They could discuss the Five Classics with humans, and debate the existence of ghosts with atheists.

The ghosts of the Six Dynasties possessed great abilities. They knew when each emperor lived, when they died, and when their kingdoms were thrown into chaos.

Men of the Six Dynasties were guided through ethereal worlds and dark hells, and returned home to write epic tales.

The Six Dynasties' men fell in love, which the ghosts also provided for them: Men attended banquets in tombs held by female ghosts.

六朝鬼魅

六朝，公元 265—588，鬼魅的数量超过了人口。活人夜晚梦见鬼魅，白天遇见鬼魅。鬼魅不避天光，犹如老鼠不避活人。六朝人的生活古古怪怪：据《幽冥录》，连鬼魅也长着汗毛、腋毛和阴毛。鬼魅与人争抢饭食。鬼魅之间打架斗殴。

六朝鬼魅有学问，可以与人论《五经》，可以与无神论者辩论有无鬼魅。

六朝鬼魅神通大，知道每一个皇帝何时生，何时死，何时天下有大乱。

六朝男人在鬼魅的帮助下，游了仙境游地府，回来之后抢小说。

六朝男人有艳福，但艳福也是鬼魅给的：女鬼们在坟中设宴，总有男人躬逢其盛。

There Six Dynasties' women would reveal their true selves and transform into white egrets and white swans. This "white" had always pulsed softly through their veins.

The white swans of the Six Dynasties were gracious. For miles and miles they chased men back and forth just to return a lost shoe.

The Six Dynasties' tigers, on the other hand, hatched their own plan. When men went outside to empty their bladders, they bit off their pricks.

The people of the Six Dynasties say that back in those days, people turning into animals was right as rain. But that miserable, old what's-his-face Kafka got it all wrong. He turned man into an animal--Twisted all around! It's written all wrong!

Translated by Unknown

六朝女人原形毕露时，就变回白鹭和白鹄，总之一个"白"字，
透着血管隐隐。
六朝白鹄心肠好，追人追出五六里，递上他丢失的鞋子。
但六朝老虎别出心裁，趁男人在屋外撒尿咬他的鸡鸡。

六朝人说，在我们那个时代，动物变人如家常便饭，可那个忧郁
的什么什么卡夫卡，少见多怪，让人变成动物——肯定是写拧了！
肯定是写错了！

2007

On FAN KUAN'S MONUMENTAL LANDSCAPE SCROLL *TRAVELERS AMONG MOUNTAINS AND STREAMS*

Looking at *Travelers among Mountains and Streams* I have to halt midair, but cannot fall.

The mountain does not need tigers and leopards for growth, or monarchs for metaphor. Guo Xi who wrote *Lofty Ambitions in Forests and Springs* would never understand.

This upright black mountain, the hard bones of existence, chest out right in my face.

The temple between the branches is so small but it should be so small; the waterfall is just a trickle but it should be just a trickle; a black mountain, not a green mountain; Fan Kuan painted with ink, with its blackness, with the five colors black comprises. People walk in daylight like nighttime. A thousand years later his brushwork of raindrops and strips are even darker.

As Fan Kuan saw it, his homeland was the landscape, therefore too the mountains and the waterfalls and the streams and the wooden bridges over the streams and the boulders and the trees and the temples and the paths and the tiny people on the paths and the mules driven by the tiny people. Those mules are four-legged birds in flight. Each tree they hobble past has attained enlightenment. Their sturdy roots grasp the earth's Shaanxi stubbornness.

题范宽巨幛山水《溪山行旅图》

观范宽《溪山行旅图》需凌空立定，且不能坠落。

大山不需借虎豹生势，亦不必凭君主喻称。后来做《林泉高致集》的郭熙永远不懂。

这直立的黑山，存在的硬骨头，胸膛挺到我的面前。

枝柯间的庙宇很小哇就该那么小；一线瀑布的清水很少呀就该那么少；黑沉沉的山，不是青山；范宽用墨，用出它的黑，用出黑中的五色。人行白昼仿佛在夜晚。一千年后他的雨点皴和条子皴更加晦暗。

在范宽看来，家国即山水，即山峰、瀑布、溪涧、溪涧上的小木桥、岩石、树木、庙宇、山道、山道上细小的人物、细小的人物驱赶的毛驴。毛驴是四条腿的小鸟在行动。它们颠儿颠儿经过的每棵大树都已得道。粗壮的树根抓住大地一派关陕的倔强。

And now Emperor Zhenzong in the capital is balancing the benefits of the elites.

And now no elite has yet to peer upon *Travelers among Mountains and Streams*. Concentrating on his almost complete masterpiece, Fan Kuan does not know he has been elevated to the ranks of "Standards from One Hundred Generations." It takes ten days to draw a rock and five to draw a river, with patience coming from enlightenment, and enlightenment not a small deal. Before you know it the Song Dynasty has attained an image: mountains like cast iron, trees like wrought iron; before you know it young Li Tang is its exemplar.

Dong Qichang didn't agree with this kind of work, saying "The artistry is too bitter." People then faked temperament, copying the ancients but completely removed from antiquity. Compared with those clever people, the ancients always come off as crude and clumsy.

Crude Fan Kuan sits on a rock alone by the river, drinking, forgetting himself. Hearing the almost inaudible sounds of a traveler on the mountain path shouting at his mule, and of rocks pressing against rocks, and of the mountain standing, and lizards aging. The black mountain before him witnesses the moment: Fan Kuan became Fan Kuan when suddenly he realized, silence can be heard.

而此刻真宗皇帝正在京城忙于平衡权贵们的利益。

而此刻任何权贵均尚未端详过这幅《溪山行旅图》。凝神这即将完成的杰作，范宽不知自己已升达"百代标程"。十日画一石五日画一水，其耐心来自悟道，而悟道是个大活。眼看大宋朝就要获得一个形象：山如铁铸，树如铁浇；眼看后人李唐将要获得一个榜样。

后人董其昌不赞成这样的工作，以为"其术太苦"。后人玩心性，虽拟古却与古人无关。与聪明的后人相比，古人总显得太憨厚，太笨拙。

憨厚的范宽独坐溪畔大石，喝酒，忘我。听见山道上旅人吆喝毛驴的几乎听不见的声音，还有岩石顶住岩石的声音、山体站立的声音、蜥蜴变老的声音。对面黑山见证了这一刻：范宽突然成为范宽当他意识到，沉寂可以被听见。

Impartial Liu Daochun said of Fan Kuan: "His tree roots are shallow, and his plains craggy." Impartial Mi Fu said of Fan Kuan: "He overused ink, so his soil and stones are indistinguishable." Impartial Su Shi said of Fan Kuan: "Though there's a bit of the old method, it's rather mundane."— Their partiality was gesticulating at great art. Their partiality was having reservations about greatness itself. They were provoked, and only unrestrained in their praise of second-rate art.

The crude man signs his name between the branches, saying little.

Translated by Lucas Klein

偏刘道醇指范宽："树根浮浅，平远多峻。"偏米芾指范宽："用墨太多，土石不分。"偏苏轼指范宽："虽稍存古法，然微有俗气。"——他们偏喜对伟大的艺术指手画脚。他们偏喜对伟大本身持保留态度。他们被刺激，只对二流艺术百分百称赞。

憨厚的人在枝柯间签上自己的名字，不多言。

2012.6.29

ONCE MORE ON FAN KUAN'S *TRAVELERS AMONG MOUNTAINS AND STREAMS*

This rock. This black rock. This black mountain. This mountain still black though upright in the sunlight. Not a green mountain, not an emerald mountain, a black mountain, an ink mountain.—But black and ink are imprecise: a murky mountain, made murkier by the aging of its silk.—Time weighs down the weight of the mountain. This heavy mountain, like a *sudden* surge, a sudden staking.—Stable, despite being a sudden staking. Was it its own idea? Or the idea of the painter? Or was the painter grabbed by such a mountain someplace in Zhongnan or Qinling? Who was there to hear Fan Kuan's gasps? On this mountain blocking sun and sky, the summit brush is tangled and dense. The brush branches are thin and hard as iron, with no bed for insects, no bed for mosquitoes or flies. Dark and clean. It fills birds with awe, leaves tigers and leopards mute or at least makes them speak in whispers, makes climbers afraid to take a leak without permission. So no one's there. No one is brave enough to climb. But in fact, this mountain could be found anywhere, with no jade, no gold, no care for itself.—No mountains care about themselves, any more than brush cares about how many flowers it will bear, or flowers care about whether they're red or pink.—Fan Kuan's flowers would be black. The color of night, the color of eyes. Who would be there to look at Fan Kuan's flowers? Fan Kuan doesn't paint flowers: because the brush is a flower, the brambles are a flower,

再题范宽《溪山行旅图》

这石头。这黑色的石头。这黑山。这矗立在阳光下却依然黑色的
山。不是青山，不是碧山，是黑山，是墨山。——但"黑"与"墨"
皆不准确：是暗沉沉的山，随绢面变旧而更加暗沉沉。——时间
加重了山体的重量感。这沉重的山，仿佛突然涌来，突然站定——
虽"突然"站定，却是稳稳地站定。是它自己的主意？抑或画家
的主意？抑或画家曾在终南山或秦岭的某处被这样的山体一把抓
住？有谁听到过范宽的惊叹？这遮天蔽日的山体，山巅灌木浓密
而细小。灌木枝子瘦硬如铁，不生虫，不生蚊蝇。黑暗而干净。
这令飞鸟敬畏，令虎豹沉默或说话时压低嗓门，令攀登者不敢擅
自方便。于是无人。无人放胆攀登。但其实，这又是随处可见之山，
不藏玉，不藏金，不关心自己。——没有任何山岭关心自己，就
像灌木不关心自己能开出多少花朵，就像花朵不关心自己是红色
还是粉色。——范宽的花朵应是黑色。是夜的颜色、眼睛的颜色。
有谁见到过范宽的花朵？范宽不画花朵：因为灌木就是花朵，荆
棘就是花朵，正如山溪就是河流，瀑布就是河流，所以范宽也不

the way the mountain stream is a river, the waterfall is a river, so Fan Kuan paints no rivers. I've seen such stinginess toward water. I've seen this trickle of waterfall to the right of the summit. I try to comprehend: this composition is not only Fan Kuan's, it is the local deity's,—thirsty nature itself. Thirsty travelers under the mountain drive thirsty mules, walking past trees whose arms are outstretched from thirst.—The echo of the mountain stream is ahead. On the right bank of the stream they can rest, even doze; they can dry their socks and clothes. And when these two stop by the stream, the breeze will give them consolation, only the breeze gives consolation, along with respect for the hardships of life. In such orthodox mountains they will encounter no enchantress carrying a basket of steamed *mantou* buns, nor will they meet the tigers, leopards, and jackals of the flying rocks and sands, though they might meet Fan Kuan, lingering in the mountains all day drinking and being enlightened, even if they can't tell what kind of person Fan Kuan might be. These two are used to the height of the mountains and the sturdiness of the trees, and the mountains and trees are accustomed to the insignificance of these travelers. Insignificant merchants in the silence of the landscape, worn and weary busybodies, not government officials or landlords. And government officials or landlords would be insignificant if they came to these mountains, too. This isn't just what Fan Kuan thinks, it's what the local deity thinks. The people in this landscape painting are almost invisible, yet it is titled *Travelers Among Mountains and Streams*.

Translated by Lucas Klein

画河流。对水的吝啬，我看到了。山峰右侧的一线瀑布，我看到了。我试图理解：这不仅是范宽的构图，这也是土地爷的构图，——这是口渴的自然本身。山下口渴的旅人赶着口渴的毛驴，走过因口渴而张开臂膀的大树。——溪水的声响在前边。溪畔大石上可以小坐，甚至小睡；可以晾袜子，晾衣服。而当这二人停在溪边的时候，必有微风送来安慰，仅有微风送来安慰，以及对艰辛生涯的敬意。他们不会在这样正派的山间遇到手提一篮馒头的妖女，也不会遇到飞沙走石的虎豹豺狼，但有可能遇到镇日盘桓山间，饮酒、悟道的范宽，而不晓范宽何许之人。这二人早已习惯了山岭的高大、树木的粗壮，而山岭和树木亦早已习惯了行人的渺小。沉寂风景中渺小的商贩，风尘仆仆的奔波者，不是官吏或地主。然即使官吏或地主来到此山间，照样渺小。这不仅是范宽的想法，这也是土地爷的想法。这是一幅几乎看不到人的山水画，却被命名为《溪山行旅图》。

2012.7.10

AFTER WANG XIMENG'S BLUE AND GREEN HORIZONTAL LANDSCAPE SCROLL, *A THOUSAND MILES OF RIVERS AND MOUNTAINS*

Green colors and blue colors flow together and form empty mountains. Some people are walking in them, but they're still empty mountains, as if the people walking there have no faces, but they are still people. No one should try to recognize themselves in these figures, or try to see the real mountains and waters of this world, nor should anyone think of trying to gain casual praise from Wang Ximeng. Wang Ximeng knows these small figures, and that not one is he himself. These are not his figures, and he cannot call out a single one by name. The figures acquire the mountains and waters, just as the mountains acquire the emerald and lapis, just as the waters acquire vastness and boats, just as Emperor Huizong got Wang Ximeng at eighteen years old, not knowing that Wang would die soon after he finished this thousand miles of rivers and mountains. The mountains and waters are nameless. Wang Ximeng realizes that people without names are just decorations in mountains and waters, just as flying birds know they are insignificant to men's games. And the birds meet in the sky. Meanwhile, people walking in the mountains have their own directions to travel and their own plans. These small figures, in white, walk, sit at leisure, go fishing, trade, surrounded by green colors and blue colors, just like, today, people, in black, go to banquets, concerts, and funerals, surrounded by golden colors and more golden colors. These small figures in white have never been born and so have never died; just

题王希孟青绿山水长卷《千里江山图》

绿色和蓝色汇集成空山。有人行走其间，但依然是空山，就像行走的人没有面孔，但依然是人。谁也别想从这些小人儿身上认出自己，就像世间的真山真水，别想从王希孟那里得到敷衍了事的赞扬。王希孟认识这些画面上的小人儿，但没有一个是他自己。这些不是他自己的小人儿，没有一个他能叫出名字。小人儿们得到山，得到水，就像山得到绿松石和青金石，水得到浩淼和船只，就像宋徽宗得到十八岁的王希孟，只是不知道他将在画完《千里江山图》之后不久便会死去。山水无名。王希孟明白，无名的人物，更只是山水的点缀，就像飞鸟明白，自己在人类的游戏中可有可无。鸟儿在空中相见。与此同时，行走在山间的人各有各的方向，各有各的打算。这些小人儿穿着白衣，行走，闲坐，打鱼，贩运，四周是绿色和蓝色，就像今天的人们穿着黑衣，出现在宴会、音乐会和葬礼之上，四周是金色和金色。这些白衣小人儿从未出生，当然也就从未死去，就像王希孟这免于污染和侵略的山水乌托邦，

like Wang Ximeng's landscape utopia, they are immune to pollution and invasion, and that is worth careful consideration. So people who are far away from social controls have no need to long for freedom, and people who haven't been destroyed by experience aren't concerned about forgetting. Wang Ximeng let the fishermen have infinite numbers of fishes to go fishing; he allowed limitless waters to run out from the mountains. According to him, happiness means the exact amount of blessing so that, immersed in the silence between mountains and waters, people can build bridges, waterwheels, roads, houses, and live quietly, just like the trees growing appropriately in the mountains, along the margins of water, or surrounding a village, and surrounding people. In the distance, the trees are like flowers. When they sway, it's the time when the clear wind is rising. When the clear wind is rising, it's time for people to sing. When people sing, it's time for an empty mountain to become an empty mountain.

Translated by Arthur Sze & the author

经得起细细的品读。远离桎梏的人啊谈不上对自由的向往，未遭
经验损毁的人啊谈不上遗忘。王希孟让打鱼的人有打不尽的鱼，
让山坳里流出流不尽的水。在他看来，幸福，就是财富的多寡恰
到好处，让人们得以在山水之间静悄悄地架桥，架水车，修路，
盖房屋，然后静悄悄地居住，就像树木恰到好处地生长在山岗、
水畔，或环绕着村落，环绕着人。远景中，树木像花儿一样。它
们轻轻摇晃，就是清风送爽的时候。清风送爽，就是有人歌唱的
时候。有人歌唱，就是空山成其为空山的时候。

2012

KHITAN MASK

The nomads and craftsmen of Khitan abut upon a sea of non-Khitan people. The sun of Khitan, its speed of rising and setting: we can only make an estimate, pretending to be one hundred per cent sure.

I chose a mouse and named it "Khitan Mouse," it's hiding right in my room. While Khitan raindrops, adapted to the vast grasslands, never ever fall on my head.

A big pair of scissors has cut off the chaotic lifeblood of the Kingdom of Khitan (This kingdom of eagles, kingdom of purebred horses and bighorn sheep); no one will ever again be responsible for the swordplay that made the illustrious name of Khitan resound everlastingly through the world.

Some remember the Khitan, only because 16th-century Europeans were once not sure whether "Khitan" and "China" denoted two separate things or whether they were two names for one country.

The "Khitan chamber pot" on the sale at the Beijing Antique Market makes the collector smile knowingly; he hears the chamber pot insistently nagging at him, "Who are Khitans?"

A guy will sometimes have his head shaved in a Khitan hairstyle: ignoramuses think him outlandish as a British punk, and the wise think him profound as an Italian monk, but he's only unintentionally disguised as a Khitan ghost.

契丹面具

契丹的游民和工匠汇入不是契丹人的人海。契丹的太阳，它上升和下降的速度，我们只能推算，假装把握十足。

我选择一只老鼠命名为"契丹老鼠"，它就躲在我的房间。而适合辽阔草原的契丹雨滴，始终不曾落在我的头顶。

一把大剪刀剪断了契丹王朝紊乱的命脉（这鹰的王朝、骏马和大角山羊的王朝）；再无人负责舞枪弄棒，保证契丹的英名能够持久震荡。

有人记得契丹，只因为 16 世纪的欧洲人曾拿不准，"契丹"和"中国"是各有所指还是一国两号。

潘家园古董市场上出售的"契丹夜壶"令古董收藏家会心一笑；他听见夜壶向他哗哗提问："谁是契丹？"

偶然有人剃出契丹发式，无知者以为他古怪如同英国朋克，有知者以为他高深如同意大利僧侣，但他实际上无意间扮作了契丹的幽魂。

...but being without the Kingdom of Khitan is like being without the Khitan princess with her amber and jade pectoral, who strummed on her crescent sword with scarlet fingernails.

Her lovely faces have been dug away from her bones by time, while what time can't dig away is this gold mask in the history museum, which is a memory of the lovely faces, over which earthworms once crawled.

Khitan has forged itself into a gold mask. All its dignity is only built upon gold but not upon Khitan calligraphy, which almost nobody can decipher now.

To history, this is barbaric, reckless, foolhardy: it seems the fake face can more effectively manage the darkness underground and the bluster above ground than the real face can.

……但是，没有了契丹王朝，就像没有了项挂琥珀璎珞的契丹公主，用染着红指甲的手指弹奏她的月牙弯刀。

她的花容被时间从骨头上挖走，而时间挖不走的，是历史博物馆里这副以她的花容为记忆、被蚯蚓爬过的黄金面具。

契丹把自己打造成一副黄金面具。它所有的尊严只建立在黄金而不是如今几乎无人能够读懂的契丹书法之上。

对历史而言这是野蛮、胆大妄为：似乎一张假脸比一张真脸能够更加有效地管理地下的黑暗和地上的大风呼啸。

Millions of rustling phantoms will kneel together around this mask. If the long-gone princess allowed, they would put on this mask in turn, take turns to stand in for the kingdom heaven never approved.

Once they had put on this mask, they couldn't see, they couldn't hear, and there'd be no way they could speak. They'd only come to the realisation of Heaven's Dao 900 years after their death.

Inside the history museum's glass case, the value of this gold mask is climbing, while its weight may be reducing from three pounds to one ounce: it might be reduced to a splendid but unreliable wrapping paper.

And maybe Khitan phantoms are rushing in to steal their princess' mask away, totally denying as they do it that there ever was a Kingdom of Khitan.

Translated by Brian Holton & Lee Man-Kay

万千幽魂会围绕这副面具齐刷刷跪倒。要是那位不复存在的公主
允许，他们会轮番戴上这副面具，轮番代表一个不曾被苍天认可
的王朝。

一戴上这副面具他们便看不见，听不见，并且有话说不出。他们
会在死后九百年悟得天道。

在历史博物馆的玻璃展柜之内，这副黄金面具的价值正在攀升，
而其重量或许正从三斤减轻为一两，减轻为一张华丽而靠不住的
包装纸。

而契丹的幽魂们或许正在赶来，要抢走他们公主的面具，同时根
本否认曾经有过契丹王朝。

2003.11

Part 2

卷二

SALUTE

One: Night

In the noise of trucks passing through the city, how hard it is to make the blood be quiet! How hard to make the draught animals be quiet! What persuasion, what promise, what bribe, what threat will make them quiet? But they are quiet.

Stone beasts under the archway are breathing moonlight. The knife grinder's rickety body is bent like the crescent moon. He is exhausted but he will not go to sleep: he whistles, to call the birds from sleep to the end of the bridge, but forgets that on the cliff, silvery as the moon, there is a pregnant leopard that no one is looking after.

The spider intercepts an imperial edict, thus going against the wish of the road.

In hemp fields, lamps have no rights of residence.

Someone is about to arrive and knock on the door, sheep are about to appear and roam in the meadow. The wind is blowing on apples which have never yet entered his dreams, a youth is singing in the basement, surpassing himself.... It's night, needless to say. Memory can create brand-new things.

致敬

一、夜

在卡车穿城而过的声音里，要使血液安静是多么难哪！要使卡车上的牲口们安静是多么难哪！用什么样的劝说，什么样的许诺，什么样的贿赂，什么样的威胁，才能使它们安静？而它们是安静的。

拱门下的石兽呼吸着月光。磨刀师傅佝偻的身躯宛如月芽。他劳累但不甘于睡眠，吹一声口哨把睡眠中的鸟儿招至桥头，却忘记了月色如银的山崖上，还有一只怀孕的豹子无人照看。

蜘蛛拦截圣旨，违背道路的意愿。

在大麻地里，灯没有居住权。

就要有人来了，来敲门；就要有羊群出现了，在草地。风吹着它从未梦见过的苹果；一个青年人在地下室里歌唱，超水平发挥……这是黑夜，还用说吗？记忆能够创造崭新的东西。

How vast the sky, higher than memory! Climb high to see far, and the spirit will know no limits. Ever-burning lamps, two or three, look like will-o'-the-wisps. For the soul that cannot sleep, there is no poetry. One needs to stay awake and be on guard, but in the face of death one cannot ponder.

I have brought you a searchlight, there must be fairy maidens flying over your head at night.

I chose this record player from the warehouse, to play you a song, to cure your old disease.

In this night, with the stars in battle-array, my hair stands on end and the black mole on the left side of my chest is blacker still. God's grain is plundered; beauty comes under attack from large, vengeful birds. On nights like this, if I fly into a rage, if I retaliate, then do not speak to me of mercy! If I pardon your crimes, then take to the road right away and do not stop to thank me.

Please clean your wounds with the juice of the ginger root.

Please leave a way out for the weasel.

How powerless the heart when the lights go out, when street-sweepers get up, when crows take off into the sunlight shining on this city, proud to have their luxurious wings no longer confused with nighttime writing.

A face flushed red, all the body's blood. The bugle blows, dust trembles: the first note always sounds bad!...

高于记忆的天空多么辽阔！登高远望，精神没有边界。三两盏长
明灯仿佛鬼火。难于入睡的灵魂没有诗歌。必须醒着，提防着，
面对死亡，却无法思索。

我给你带来了探照灯，你的头上夜晚定有仙女飞行。

我从仓库中选择了这架留声机，为你播放乐曲，为你治疗沉疾。

在这星星布阵的夜晚，我的头发竖立，我左胸上的黑痣更黑。上
帝的粮食被抢掠；美，被愤愤不平的大鸟袭击。在这样的夜晚，
如果我发怒，如果我施行报复，就别跟我谈论悲慈！如果我赦免
你们，就赶紧走路，不必称谢。

请用姜汁擦洗伤口。

请给黄鼠狼留一条生路。

心灵多么无力，当灯火熄灭，当扫街人起床，当乌鸦迎着照临本
城的阳光起飞，为它们华贵的翅膀不再混同于夜间的文字而自豪。

通红的面孔，全身的血液：铜号吹响了，尘埃战栗；第一声总是
难听的！

Two: Salute

Dejection. Dangling gongs and drums. Dozing leopard in the basement. Spiral staircase. Nighttime torch. City gates. Cold, below the ancient stars and reaching to the grass's roots. Sealed-off body. Undrinkable water. Tears unformed. Punishment unbegun. Chaos. Equilibrium. Ascension. A blank.... How does one speak of dejection and not be in the wrong? Face to face with a crown of flowers left at the crossroads, please realize the price one pays for recklessness!

Pain: a sea, unmovable.

To want to scream, to force the steel to shed a tear, to force the mice used to living in secret to line up and appear before me. To want to scream, but in the softest possible voice, not like curses but like prayers, not like the roar of cannon but like the whistle of the wind. A stronger heartbeat accompanies a greater silence, helplessly watching how the stored-up rain will all be drunk—well then, scream! Oh, how I want to scream, with hundreds of crows clamoring. I have no mouth of gold, no words of jade—I am an omen of no good.

Too many desires, too little saltwater.

Illusions depend on capital for their preservation.

Let the rose redress our errors, let thunder reprimand us! On this endless road, there is no asking where the journey leads. When the moth flies into the flame, that is no time to talk of eternity and it is hard to find proof of a man's moral flawlessness.

二、致敬

苦闷。悬挂的锣鼓。地下室中昏睡的豹子。旋转的楼梯。夜间的火把。城门。古老星座下触及草根的寒冷。封闭的肉体。无法饮用的水。似大船般漂移的冰块。作为乘客的鸟。阻断的河道。未诞生的儿女。未成形的泪水。未开始的惩罚。混乱。平衡。上升。空白……怎样谈论苦闷才不算过错？面对岔道上遗落的花冠，请考虑铤而走险的代价！

痛苦：一片搬不动的大海。

在苦难的第七页书写着文明。

多想叫喊，迫使钢铁发出回声，迫使习惯于隐秘生活的老鼠列队来到我的面前。多想叫喊，但要尽量把声音压低，不能像谩骂，而应像祈祷，不能像大炮的轰鸣，而应像风的呼啸。更强烈的心跳伴随着更大的寂静，眼看存贮的雨水即将被喝光，叫喊吧！啊，我多想叫喊，当数百只乌鸦聒噪，我没有金口玉言——我就是不祥之兆。

欲望太多，海水太少。

幻想靠资本来维持。

让玫瑰纠正我们的错误，让雷霆对我们加以训斥！在漫漫旅途中，不能追问此行的终点。在飞蛾扑火的一刹那，要谈论永恒是不合时宜的，要寻找证据来证明一个人的白璧无瑕是困难的。

Memory: my textbook.

Love: unfinished worries.

A man goes deep into the mountains and miraculously survives. In winter he hoards cabbage, in summer he makes ice. He says: "One who will let nothing move him is not real, neither where he comes from nor in his present life." Therefore we crowd around the peach blossom to sharpen our sense of smell. Face to face with the peach blossom and other things of beauty, one who knows not how to doff his hat in salute is not our comrade.

But we do not hope for an outcome in which souls are made to lie idle and words blackmailed.

Poetry guides the dead and the next generation.

记忆：我的课本。

爱情：一件未了的心事。

一个走进深山的人奇迹般地活着。他在冬天储存白菜，他在夏天制造冰。他说："无从感受的人是不真实的，连同他的祖籍和起居。"因此我们凑近桃花以磨练嗅觉。面对桃花以及其他美丽的事物，不懂得脱帽致敬的人不是我们的同志。

但这不是我们盼待的结果：灵魂，被闲置；词语，被敲诈。

诗歌教导了死者和下一代。

Three: Abode

Clocks let on the sounds and sights of spring, the cricket on its manor sings. What I will not allow has happened: I am slowly changing into someone else. I must call out three times, I must call myself back.

With the props that I've collected, I decorate the room. Every night, I have the good fortune to enjoy a play staged purely by props.

The kitchen is a place of knives and forks to sleep, the square is a place for the goddess to stand.

The world in the mirror is my world's equal but its opposite, too: if it isn't hell, it must be heaven. A man exactly like me, but my opposite too, lives in that world: if he isn't Lucan he must be Saint John.

I rarely touch my cheeks or my ankles. I rarely touch myself. Therefore I rarely criticize myself, either, and I rarely beat myself up.

This often happens: Liu Jun makes a phone call to find another Liu Jun. As if I am talking to myself, cradling the phone.

The smile of one who suffers from a mental illness. The reproductive organ he bares to the sun and to women. The sound of him banging his head against the wall. His underdeveloped brain. "Am I right? Am I right?"—the question he persists in asking, over and over again.

There is no guard at the door of my house. If I hire a guard, I must guard him with all my might.

三、居室

钟表吐露春光，蟋蟀在它自己的领地歌唱。不允许的事情发生了：
我渐渐变成别人。我必须大叫三声，叫回我自己。

我用收集的道具装饰房间。每天夜晚，我都有幸观赏一场纯粹由
道具上演的戏剧。

厨房适于刀叉睡眠，广场适于女神站立。

镜中的世界与我的世界完全对等但又完全相反，那不是地狱就是
天堂；一个与我一模一样但又完全相反的男人，在那个世界里生
活，那不是武松就是西门庆。

我很少摸到我的脸颊、我的脚踝。我很少摸到我自己。因此我也
很少批评我自己，我也很少殴打我自己。

常常有这样的事情发生：刘军打电话寻找另一个刘军。就像我抱
着电话机自言自语。

精神病患者的微笑。他暴露给太阳和女人的生殖器。他以头撞墙
的声音。他发育不良的大脑。"对不对——对不对？"——他反
复追问的问题。

我的家没有守门人。如果我雇一个守门人，我就得全力以赴守住
他。

If three thousand beauties came to sit in this room, would you be excited or afraid? Three thousand beauties, they might be three thousand fox spirits, the only way to cope with them would be to get them drunk.

A man whose axe has chopped his fingers off comes to tell me the story of his love.

Experiences of others may to us well be taboos.

The lilac in the ink well is slowly turning blue. It hopes to remember this night, it would do anything to remember this night, but that is impossible.

I nourish this flower seed with my innermost secret: when the lotus blooms, it will be summer.

如果这房间坐进美女三千，你是兴奋还是恐惧？美女三千，或许是三千只狐狸精，对付她们的唯一办法是将她们灌醉。

一个曾以利斧断指的男人，来向我讲述他的爱情故事。

别人的经验往往成为我们的禁忌。

墨水瓶里的丁香花渐渐发蓝。它希望记住今夜，它拼命要记住今夜。但这是不可能的。

我用内心的秘密滋养这莲子：一旦荷花开放，就是夏季。

Four: The Monster

The monster—I have seen it. The monster has bristly hair, razor-sharp teeth, it is close to going blind. The monster breathes its husky breath, it shouts of calamity, yet its feet move without a sound. The monster has no sense of humor, like someone trying hard to cover up humble origins, like someone destroyed by a calling; it has no cradle offering memories, no goal offering direction, not enough lies to defend itself. It beats on tree trunks, it collects infants; it lives like a rock, it dies like an avalanche.

The crow seeks allies among scarecrows.

The monster hates my hairdo, hates my smell, hates my regret and my overcautious ways. In short, it hates my habit of dressing up happiness in pearls and jade. It bursts through my door, tells me to stand in a corner, will not let me explain and falls through my chair, shatters my mirror, rips my curtains and all protective screens around my private soul. I beg it: "When I am thirsty, don't take away my teacup!" Right then and there it digs out water from a spring: that must be its answer.

A ton of parrots, a ton of parrot-talk!

For the tiger we say 'tiger,' for the donkey we say 'donkey.' But how do you address the monster? It has no name, so its flesh melts into its shadow, so you cannot call out to it, so you cannot determine its place in the sun nor foretell the fortune or misfortune it may bring. It should be given a name, like 'sorrow' or 'shame,' it should be given a pond from which to drink, it should be given a roof over its head for shelter from the rain. A monster with no name is scary.

四、巨兽

那巨兽，我看见了。那巨兽，毛发粗硬，牙齿锋利，双眼几乎失明。那巨兽，喘着粗气，嘟囔着厄运，而脚下没有声响。那巨兽，缺乏幽默感，像竭力掩盖其贫贱出身的人，像被使命所毁掉的人，没有摇篮可资回忆，没有目的地可资向往，没有足够的谎言来为自我辩护。它拍打树干，收集婴儿；它活着，像一块岩石，死去，像一场雪崩。

乌鸦在稻草人中间寻找同伙。

那巨兽，痛恨我的发型，痛恨我的气味，痛恨我的遗憾和拘谨。一句话，痛恨我把幸福打扮得珠光宝气。它挤进我的房门，命令我站立在墙角，不由分说坐垮我的椅子，打碎我的镜子，撕烂我的窗帘和一切属于我个人的灵魂屏障。我哀求它："在我口渴的时候别拿走我的茶杯！"它就地掘出泉水，算是对我的回答。

一吨鹦鹉，一吨鹦鹉的废话！

我们称老虎为"老虎"，我们称毛驴为"毛驴"。而那巨兽，你管它叫什么？没有名字，那巨兽的肉体和阴影便模糊一片，你便难以呼唤它，你便难以确定它在阳光下的位置并预卜它的吉凶。应该给它一个名字，比如"哀愁"或者"羞涩"，应该给它一片饮水的池塘，应该给它一间避雨的屋舍。没有名字的巨兽是可怕的。

A thrush bumps off all the king's men!

The monster is exposed to temptations too, but not those of the palace, not those of female beauty and not those of sumptuous candle-lit banquets. It is coming toward us, but surely there is nothing about us to make its mouth water? Surely it will not try to suck emptiness from our bodies? What kind of temptation is that! Sideways through a shadowy passageway, the monster collides head-on with a glint of steel, and that smallest of injuries teaches it to moan—to moan, to live, not to know what faith is. But as soon as it calms down, it hears the sesame stalks budding once again, it smells the Chinese rose's fragrance once again.

Across a thousand mountains flies the wild goose, too timid to speak of itself.

This metaphor of a monster goes down the mountainside, picks flowers, sees the reflection of its face in the rivers, in its heart of hearts feels unsure who that is; then it swims across, goes ashore, looks back at the haze about the water, finds nothing, understands nothing; then it charges into the city, follows the trail of a girl, comes by a piece of meat, spends the night under eaves, dreams of a village, of a companion; then it sleepwalks fifty miles, knows no fear, wakes up in the morning sun, discovers it has returned to its earlier place of departure: still that thick bed of leaves, hidden underneath the leaves still the dagger—what is about to happen here?

Dove in the sand, you are awakened by the shine of blood: the time to fly has come!

一只画眉把国王的爪牙全干掉！

它也受到诱惑，但不是王宫，不是美女，也不是一顿丰饶的烛光晚宴。它朝我们走来，难道我们身上有令它垂涎欲滴的东西？难道它要从我们身上啜饮空虚？这是怎样的诱惑呵！侧身于阴影的过道，迎面撞上刀光，一点点伤害使它学会了的呻吟——呻吟，生存，不知信仰为何物；可一旦它安静下来，便又听见芝麻拔节的声音，便又闻到月季的芳香。

飞越千山的大雁，羞于谈论自己。

这比喻的巨兽走下山坡，采摘花朵，在河边照见自己的面影，内心疑惑这是谁；然后泅水渡河，登岸，回望河上雾霭，无所发现亦无所理解；然后闯进城市，追踪少女，得到一块肉，在屋檐下过夜，梦见一座村庄、一位伴侣；然后梦游五十里，不知道害怕，在清晨的阳光里醒来，发现回到了早先出发的地点：还是那厚厚的一层树叶，树叶下面还藏着那把匕首——有什么事情要发生？

沙土中的鸽子，你由于血光而觉悟。
啊，飞翔的时代来临了！

Five: Maxims

Strike down shadows, and it will be people that stand up.

Trees listen to trees, birds listen to birds; when poisonous snakes raise their bodies upright to attack people passing, they become people themselves.

To scrutinize the face in the mirror is to affront a stranger.

The law says: those who go looting at the scene of a fire must die, those who put up a sheep's head to sell dog meat must get what they deserve, those who gaze and peer to left and right will find a trap beneath their feet, those with narrow chicken minds must meet with scorn. But I can't stop myself from adding something here, for I have seen that women whose star is rising are just as competent as men whose star is rising, just as muscular, just as ruthless.

The sunflower is after all a flower too.

Why have cats not tigers become our pets?

Tiny pain, like the feeling of sand pouring into one's eye socket—from whom does one seek compensation?

五、箴言

击倒一个影子，站起一个人。

树木倾听着树木，鸟雀倾听着鸟雀；当一条毒蛇直立起身体，攻击路人，它就变成了一个人。

你端详镜中的面孔，这是对于一个陌生人的冒犯。

法律上说：那趁火打劫的人必死，那挂羊头卖狗肉的人必遭报应，那东张西望的人陷阱就在脚前，那小肚鸡肠的人必遭唾弃。而我不得不有所补充，因为我看到飞黄腾达的猴子像飞黄腾达的人一样能干，一样肌肉发达，一样不择手段。

葵花居然也是花！

为什么是猫而不是老虎成了我们的宠物？

A book will change me, if I want to take it in; a girl will change me, if I want to sing her praises; a road will change me, if I walk it to the end; a coin will change me, if I want to own it. If I change someone else who lives beside me, I change myself: my single conscience makes the both of us suffer, my single selfishness makes us both blush.

Truth cannot be public. Thoughts without echo are difficult to sing.

Anger puts incantations out of order.

To the shipwrecked sailor, what use is a compass?

Don't ask too much of the world; don't sleep with your wife in your arms while dreaming of high profits; don't light lamps during the day, don't do business with the night; smearing black on other faces will not make your face any whiter. Remember: don't piss in the wilderness; don't sing in cemeteries; don't make rash promises; don't be a nuisance; make wisdom into something useful.

Motionless shadows may be held in contempt, but one must stand in awe of moving shadows.

The sunbirds all suddenly take off, who is giving chase?

What kind of luck will make your left eye-lid stop twitching?

小小的疼痛，像沙子涌入眼眶的感觉——向谁索取赔偿呢？

一本书将改变我，如果我想要领会它；一个姑娘将改变我，如果我想要赞美她；一条道路将改变我，如果我想要走完它；一枚硬币将改变我，如果我想要占有它。我改变另一个生活在我身旁的人，也改变自己；我一个人的良心使我们两人受苦，我一个人的私心杂念使我们两人脸红。

真理不能公开，没有回声的思想难于歌唱。

愤怒使咒语失灵。

对于海上落难的水手，给他罗盘何用？

不要向世界要求得太多。不要搂着妻子睡眠，同时梦想着高额利润。不要在白天点灯。不要给别人的脸上抹黑。记住：不要在旷野里撒尿。不要在墓地里高歌。不要轻许诺言。不要惹人讨厌。让智慧成为有用的东西。

可以蔑视静止的阴影，但必须对移动的阴影保持敬畏。

太阳鸟争飞，谁在驱赶？

什么样的好运才能终止你左眼皮不住的跳动？

Six: Ghosts

The air embraces us, but we have never noticed. The dead have withdrawn from us, into the fields, into the moonlight, but we know exactly where they are—in their joy they will not run farther than a child.

The treasures buried deep and unknown to anyone have all been spent by Time, with nothing in return.
The dead buried deep and gradually forgotten—how can they take care of themselves? They should be moved out of their graves.

The death of others makes us guilty.

Sorrowful winds surround the dead and ask for consolation.

There is to be no death by lightning, no death by drowning, no death by poison, no death by battle, no death by disease, no death by accident, no death by unending laughter or unending crying or gluttonous eating and gluttonous drinking or an unstoppable flow of words until one's strength is exhausted. Well—how then is one to die? Noble death, ugly corpses; a death without a corpse is impossible.

六、幽灵

空气拥抱我们，但我们向未觉察；死者远离我们，在田野中，在月光下，但我们确知他们的所在——他们高兴起来，不会比一个孩子跑得更远。

那些被埋藏很深并且无人知晓的财富，被时间花掉了，没有换取任何东西。那些被埋藏很深并且渐被忘却的死者，怎能照顾好自己？应该将他们从坟穴挪出。

他人的死使我们负罪。

悲伤的风围住死者索要安慰。

不能死于雷击，不能死于溺水，不能死于毒药，不能死于械斗，不能死于疾病，不能死于事故，不能死于大笑不止或大哭不止或暴饮暴食或滔滔不绝的谈说，直到力量用尽。那么如何死去呢？崇高的死亡，丑陋的尸体：不留下尸体的死亡是不可能的。

We break up roads and build high rises to make the ghosts lose their way.

Things left behind by the dead sit in a circle, holding their breath and waiting to be used.

How will the ghosts appear? Unless hats can be transformed into hat ghosts and clothes be transformed into clothes ghosts, flesh-turned-ghost must be naked, but the appearance of naked ghosts is not in keeping with our current morality.

In the dark, someone reaches out a finger and taps me on the nose.

The tinkle of the devil's chimes is just what I need.

我们翻修街道，起造高楼，为了让幽灵迷路。

那些死者的遗物围坐成一圈，屏住呼吸，等待被使用。

幽灵将如何显现呢？除非帽子可以化作帽子的幽灵，衣服可以化作衣服的幽灵，否则由肉转化的幽灵必将赤裸，而赤裸的幽灵显现，不符合我们存在的道德。

黑暗中有人伸出手指刮我的鼻子。

魔鬼的铃声，恰好被我所利用。

Seven: Fourteen Dreams

I dream of lying on my back with a sparrow standing on my chest telling me: "I am your soul!"

I dream of a swimming pool lined with sheets of iron. I lie flat, singing to my heart's content while my feet are kicking the iron and keeping time, but suddenly there is no one left in the pool.

In my dreams I steal things. How can I protest my innocence to the sun?

I dream of a pile of letters on my doorstep. I stoop to pick one up. But this is a love letter I wrote to a girl, years ago! Why has she returned it?

I dream of a woman calling me on the phone. A stranger, a woman who seems as if she is already dead, in a tone of utmost concern urges me not to attend tonight's party.

I dream of vanishing from the face of the earth. In a subway station, I hear an old lady sobbing.

I dream of Haizi, grinning at me and denying his death.

I dream of Luo Yihe luring me into a garage, its floor covered in oil stains. In a corner stands a single bed with white sheets. This is where he sleeps, every night.

七、十四个梦

我梦见我躺着，一只麻雀站在我的胸脯上对我说："我就是你的灵魂！"

我梦见一座游泳池，四周围着铁板。我伏在铁板上纵情歌唱，我的脚在铁板上踢出节拍，而游泳池内忽然空无一人。

我在梦中偷盗。我怎样向太阳解释我的清白？

我梦见一堆书信堆在我的门前。我弯腰拾起其中的一封。哦，那是我多年以前写给一个姑娘的情书！她为什么归还？

我梦见一个女人给我打来电话。一个陌生的女人，一个似乎已经死去的女人，以关怀备至的口吻劝告我，不要去参加今晚的晚会。

我梦见我从地面上消逝。在地铁车站，我听见一个老太婆的抽泣声。

我梦见海子嬉皮笑脸地向我否认他的死亡。

我梦见骆一禾把我引进一间油渍满地的车库。在车库的一角摆着一张铺着白色床单的单人床。他就睡在那里，每天晚上。

I dream of entering a meeting room, the air inside thick with smoke. The room is full of men and women seated in chairs, with blurred faces, not saying a word. As I sit down, a man comes storming through the door, his face covered in blood, screaming and shouting: "Who's the traitor?"

I dream of a child falling from a high rise. Without wings.

I have dreamt of twisted steel. I have dreamt of poisonous leaves — this is a city in the midst of collapse; fires rage, hooded men emerge and vanish. But one small building is left in peace. I am keeping my appointment, sitting on the stone steps outside the entrance, but the person I'm expecting never shows up.

What kind of horse is called a 'Horse of Fortune'?

What kind of meteor will set the sea on fire?

I dream of lying on my back, the waves outside my window crashing ever louder. On this solitary island even the seagulls have nowhere to roost, but who is that man, whose face is the face that flashes past my window?

我梦见我走进一间乌烟瘴气的会议室。会议室里坐满了面孔模糊、一言不发的男人和女人。我坐下，这时一个满脸是血的男人闯进门来，大呼小叫："谁是叛徒？"

我梦见一个孩子从高楼坠落。没有翅膀。

我梦见了变形的钢铁，我梦见了有毒的树叶——这是一座城市在崩塌：大火熊熊，蒙面人出没。但一座小楼却安然无恙；我没有失约，我坐在楼门口的石阶上，但我等待的那个人始终没有出现。

什么样的马叫做"小吉星马"？

什么样的陨石使大海燃烧？

我梦见我躺着，窗外海浪的喧声一阵猛似一阵。这座孤岛上连海鸥也无法栖息，而那个闪现于窗口的男人的面孔是谁呢？

Eight: Winter

This is the time when the hair turns grey, this is the time when Orion passes by us, this is the time when the soul loses its water and the snow descends on the factory's reception office. A girl sitting down is invited and takes to the dance floor in flickering light, a spare-time writer stops writing and starts to prepare food for the birds of dawn.

Snow is falling, horse dung is freezing.
Village accountants are dancing into the city.
A cat stops on route and enters into debate with itself, in two voices.
A painting incomprehensible to the child remains incomprehensible to this day.

The taxi covered in snow is pure white, like a polar bear. Its engine doesn't work, its body temperature drops to zero. But I can't stand watching it give up, so I write "I love you" on one of its windows. As my finger moves across the glass, it makes a happy, squeaking sound, just like the face of a girl expecting a kiss will start to glow.

Diseases do not go around in the winter, diseases do as they please.

Frozen taps save on every drop of water, frozen oceans save on our deaths.

八、冬

这是头发变白的时候，这是猎户座从我们身旁经过的时候，这是灵魂失去水分，而大雪落向工厂传达室的时候，一个座位上的姑娘受到邀请，走下灯光变幻的舞池，一个业余作者停止写作，开始为黎明的鸟雀准备食品。

雪在下，马粪被冻硬。乡村会计跳舞进城。

一只猫停在中途，用两种声音自我辩论。

一幅小时候看不懂的画至今依然无法看懂。

那部盖在雪下的出租汽车洁白得像一头北极熊。它的发动机坏了，体温下降到零。但我不忍心目睹它自暴自弃，便在车窗上写下"我爱你"。当我的手指划在玻璃上，它愉快地发出"吱吱"响，仿佛一个姑娘，等待着接吻，额头上放光。

疾病不在冬天里流行，疾病有它自己的打算。

被冻住的水龙头，节约了每一滴水；冰封的大海，节约了我们的死亡。

Whenever I wake up in the dead of night, that is when the fire in the stove goes out. Barefoot, I get out of bed, walk toward the fire-stove, rattle the fire-tongs, and fire-flames—gone without saying goodbye—come crackling back into this world to warm the night's saliva and breath. For the one just now dreaming of wolves, my lighting the fire means rescue. How I want to tell him that even in the midst of cold, fire will burn one's hand; wolves' fear of fire must go back to when one among them was burnt by fire.

Oh you hero who break through my door, you can take the money-jar from under my bed, take the fire from my stove, but you cannot have my glasses and you cannot have my slippers—you can't live in this world pretending to be me.

An address with no name has made me silent for a long time, a face has been forgotten: another life, another way of killing time, have formed an other of my flesh and blood. With the address in my hand, I walk into a street full of wind and snow: by what sort of people shall I be admitted, rejected?

Spit marks: there are people living here.

The cold has underrated our endurance.

Translated by Maghiel van Crevel

每次我在半夜醒来，都是炉火熄灭的时候。我赤脚下床，走向火炉，弄响火钳，那不辞而别的火焰便又噼噼啪啪地回来，温暖这世界黑夜的口水和呼吸。对于那恰好梦见狼群的人，我生火是救了他。我多想告诉他，即使是在寒冷的中心，火焰也是烫手的；狼群惧怕火焰，一定是由于它们中间有谁曾被火焰烫伤。

哦，破门而入的好汉，你可以拿走我床底的钱罐，你可以拿走我炉中的火焰，但你不能拿走我的眼镜、我的拖鞋——你不能冒充我活在这世上。

一个不具姓名的地址使我沉默良久，一张面孔被我忘却：另一种生活，另一种排遣时间的方法，构成了我的另一部分血肉。我手持地址走上风雪弥漫的大街，我将被什么人接纳或拒绝？

痰迹，有人生存。

寒冷低估了我们的耐力。

1992

WHAT THE EAGLE SAYS

One: Of Thinking, As Harmful As It Is Fearful

1/ I have heard it said that in some village, some disease has made all people's brains rot away, and the village chief is alone in that only half his brain is dead. That is why people often hurry to his home in the middle of the night, drag him from his bed and yell at him: "Think this matter over for me!"

2/ You see, thinking is a burden, and damages one's dignity.

3/ I have heard it said that once there was a boy who, in order to think nonsense, used to hide in iron pots and birds' nests, while his mother was convinced that he could not run from the hollow of her hand. Until one day he disappeared completely: then even he did not know where he found himself, to say nothing of his worried mother.

4/ You see, thinking really is as harmful as it is fearful.

5/ (Whatever can be called "an evil habit" fascinates and addicts people.)

6/ One of my ancestors wrote a memorandum to the ruler proposing to forbid all thinking, which the ruler happily accepted. But ere long he decided to postpone its implementation, and first of all to forbid nudity in one's own home.

7/ He was wrong. This shows his lack of thinking. For no one dares be sure that when he pushes the gate of thinking open, a beautiful woman will come out and not a tiger; no one dares be sure that beautiful women cannot roar and tigers know no tenderness.

8/ That is why thinking is not as good as amusement! That is why the pill roller has invented sleeping pills. Sleeping pills can exorcise the thinking devil, it's just that pill bottles never say so.

鹰的话语

一、关于思想既有害又可怕

1. 我听说，在某座村庄，所有人的脑子都因某种疾病而坏死，只有村长的脑子坏掉一半。因此常有人半夜跑到村长家，从床上拽起他来并且喝令："给我想想此事！"

2. 你看思想是一种负担，有损于尊严。

3. 我听说，曾有一个男孩惯于为胡思乱想而藏进铁锅或鸟窝，而他母亲确信他跑不出自己的掌心。直到有一天，他彻底消失：连他自己亦不知他身在何方，更不用说他焦虑的母亲。

4. 你看思想的确既有害又可怕。

5. （那可以被称之为"恶习"的，无不使人着迷和过瘾。）

6. 我的祖先曾上书他的君王建议禁止思想，君王欣然接受。但时隔不久他又决定暂缓实行。他决定首先禁止人们在家中赤身裸体。

7. 他错了。这表明他缺乏思想。因为没有人敢肯定当他推开思想之门时，从里面出来的是美女而不是老虎；没有人敢肯定美女不会咆哮而老虎没有柔情。

8. 因此与其思想不如逗笑！因此药剂师发明了安眠药。安眠药可驱逐思想的魔鬼，只是任何药瓶上都不曾注明。

9/ On a sleepless night I hear someone shout my name. Chasing the shouts through storms and high water I can barely hold my footing, but fail to chase anyone down. That is why I observe that I am becoming bewitched.

10/ Therefore I walk close to the buildings, as if in my breast I were carrying the key to a treasure vault. I keep looking over my shoulder for one who may be treading on my heel, until I bump into a tree, until I bump into another one that walks as if in his breast he were carrying the key to a treasure vault.

11/ I believe that I am on the wrong track: finding pleasure in refuting my self. Refutation by the self will always displease another. Fortunately, the one I refute is my self.

12/ In the mirror I can see myself, but not my thinking: as soon as I see my thinking, it stagnates.

Two: Of Loneliness, That Is Desire Unsatisfied

13/ The moon breeds desire for emotion, onions breed desire for copulation, herbal cures breed desire for affliction, flames breed desire for death. When I deal with desire for a meal, I cannot tell if it originates in me or in the roundworms in my belly. Of the roundworms, I cannot tell if they partake in my lively consciousness.

14/ Faced with desire even a king will stand at attention, subject to desire even a fool will show his cunning. Although you do not know what it is vanished in the wind, you know but all too well that your desirous hands stay empty: hence, you enter the gate of loneliness.

9. 在一个失眠之夜我听到有人喊我的名字。我追踪这喊声，逆风涉水，险些滑倒，却没有追上任何人。我因此断定这是我着魔的开始。

10. 为此我溜着墙根走路，有似怀揣一把金库的钥匙。我不断回头寻找那个可能跟踪我的人，直到撞上一棵树，直到撞上另一个有似怀揣金库钥匙的人。

11. 我想我已误入歧途：以反驳自己为乐事。当我自行反驳时总有他人不乐意，幸好我反驳的是自己。

12. 我在镜中看到我自己，但看不到我的思想；一旦我看到我的思想，我的思想就停滞。

二、关于孤独即欲望得不到满足

13. 月亮激发情欲，洋葱激发性欲，草药激发生病欲，火焰激发死亡欲。至于食欲，我说不清它源于我还是我肚子里的蛔虫。至于蛔虫，我说不清它们是否参与我活跃的意识。

14. 在欲望的面前君王也要立正，在欲望的支配下傻瓜也要显示他的精明。尽管你并不知道有什么东西随风而逝，但你却知道你欲望的双手空空：你由此进入孤独之门。

15/ You could give up your house in order to test your perseverance. But when, tired of hardship, you want to summon your joys anew, you discover that in the house the mice have now established their system: hence, you enter the gate of loneliness.

16/ You could doubt yourself more every day, and thereupon begin to punish yourself blindly. As if you had personally planted a skinny apple tree, only to be knocked unconscious by a plenitude of falling apples (they had mistaken you for Newton): hence, you enter the gate of loneliness.

17/ You could with a hypocritical mouth denounce a hypocritical world. Either you are wrong, or the world is wrong. You force upon yourself a bright red face and mute speechlessness, showing your sincerity: hence, you enter the gate of loneliness.

18/ You could fabricate a mission in life and set out to work for it, like an underground worker. But in the end your mission in life threatens to take your life: hence, you enter the gate of loneliness.

19/ Loneliness, labyrinth of the self. Inside the labyrinth, plants blossom not in order to seduce, not in order to sell (their aim is elsewhere): as a result one does not see the plants cheer, one does not see them sing or dance (howso, then, may their inner joy be discerned?).

20/ If you keep a bird you turn the labyrinth into a birdcage; if you keep a dog you turn the labyrinth into a doghouse. If you want to deny that you are yourself a bird, right then you are vying for food with that bird; if you want to deny that you are yourself a dog, all you are left with is to bark, just like a dog.

21/ Lonely one in danger, do your haemorrhoids still hurt? The pain reminds us that time is not a supposition but the loss of rhythm in the blob, of the machine's rotational speed, of friction between man and woman, of brainpower. Continuous applause exhorts the lonely one to skate on across dangerous ice.

15. 或为一试耐力你放弃你的房屋。而当你厌倦了困苦想重新招回你的欢娱，却发现那房屋中已建立起老鼠们的制度：你由此进入孤独之门。

16. 或你自我怀疑日甚一日，于是开始了盲目的自我惩罚。这正如你亲手栽下一棵皮包骨的苹果树，却被下落的丰满的苹果砸晕（苹果错把你当成了牛顿）：你由此进入孤独之门。

17. 或你用一张虚伪的嘴声讨一个虚伪的世界。要么你错了，要么世界错了。你把自己逼到满脸通红、哑口无言的地步，真诚便出现：你由此进入孤独之门。

18. 或你编造一项使命，并为此而工作，像一个地下工作者。但这项使命最终威胁要你的命：你由此进入孤独之门。

19. 孤独，自我的迷宫。在这迷宫里，植物开花却不是为了勾引，不是为了出售（它另有目的）；植物结果却不见它欢呼，不见它歌舞（这内在的喜悦何由辨识）。

20. 你养了一只鸟就把这迷宫变成一只鸟笼；你养了一条狗就把这迷宫变成一个狗窝。当你想否认自己是一只鸟时你正在与鸟争论；当你想否认自己是一条狗时你只好像狗一样吠叫。

21. 危险的孤独者，你的痔疮还疼吗？这疼痛提醒我们时间不是假设而是血流的节奏、机器的转速、夫妇之间的磨擦和脑力的耗损。经久不息的掌声鼓励孤独者在危险的冰面上继续滑行。

22/ Because you have missed the party you make it in time for a fight. Because you have not managed to become a saint you get drunk as a lord, in the street. You are singing, others think you are screaming. You make demands, but in the end you sacrifice yourself. A bloke following your tracks ends up together with you, falling in the trap.

23/ Loneliness has giant proportions.

24/ The labyrinth of loneliness is overcrowded.

25/ Shall we not read the map? At sorrow lies the first crossroads, with a road to song and a road to bewilderment; at bewilderment lies the second crossroads, with a road to pleasure and a road to nothingness; at nothingness lies the third crossroads, with a road to death and a road to insight; at insight lies the fourth crossroads, with a road to madness and a road to silence.

Three: Of False Causality and Real Coincidence in the Dark Room

26/ In the dark room, I put my ear to the wall and listen intently, but hear not a sound from the neighbors on the other side—but suddenly I hear someone on the other side put their ear to the wall too. I quickly recall mine, and control myself like a man of good behavior.

27/ In the dark room, I should not wake from a sweet dream when my father wakes from an evil dream. He berates me, and in berating me is right: I rack my brains, hoping to reconcile social loyalty and filial piety. I tell him my sweet dream so he can dream it in turn, but he forgets it in the washroom.

22. 你因错过一场宴会而赶上一场斗殴。你因没能成为圣贤而在街头喝得烂醉。你歌唱，别人以为你在尖叫。你索取，最终将自己献出。一个跟踪你的家伙与你一起掉进陷阱。

23. 孤独有一个庞大的体积。

24. 在孤独的迷宫里人满为患。

25. 要不要读一下这张地图？忧伤是第一个岔路口：一条路通向歌唱，一条路通向迷惘；迷惘是第二个岔路口：一条路通向享乐，一条路通向虚无；虚无是第三个岔路口：一条路通向死亡，一条路通向彻悟；彻悟是第四个岔路口：一条路通向疯狂，一条路通向寂静。

三、关于黑暗房间里的假因果真偶然

26. 在黑暗的房间，我附耳于墙，倾听，但听不到隔壁邻居家的任何响动。但我忽然听到隔壁也有人附耳于墙。我赶紧把耳朵收回，约束自己做一个品行端正的人。

27. 在黑暗的房间，我不该醒自一个好梦，当我父亲醒自一个噩梦。他训斥我一顿，他训斥得有理；我深深反省，以期忠孝两全。我把好梦讲给他，让他再做一遍，可他把这好梦忘在了洗手间。

28/ After an ascetic has narrowly escaped death he turns into a playboy.

29/ A brilliant lad murders two other brilliant lads, for the sole reason that all three look alike.

30/ In the dark room, I carry on like gods and devils. And verily a nitwit enters and kneels before me. With one kick I shove him aside, and continue to indulge in pleasure, and another nitwit bursts through the door, waving a cleaver to cut my life short.

31/ In the dark room, I turn on the radio. My self-pity is aroused by a theatrical love story. At that moment a burglar comes crawling from under my bed, who first discusses the meaning of life with me, then pledges to become a new man.

32/ An expert on Confucius' Analects argues with yet another expert on Confucius' Analects until his skin hangs down in shreds.

33/ Du Fu has been praised so much that yet another Du Fu is sure to end up empty-handed.

34/ In the dark room, I once flattered a dead man. He was not my ancestor but my neighbor. I made up a splendid life for him, and his ashen face blushed scarlet. Years later, I sit down to a sumptuous table in the home of his grandson.

35/ In the dark room, I invent the portrait of a girl. A friend says he knows the girl in the painting. She lives in the Eastern part of town, at 35 Spring Grass Alley. Once I have found the address, her neighbors say she has just set out on a long journey.

36/ For the excited grave-robber faced with a grave robbed clean, there is nothing to do.

37/ The cook for whom there is nothing to do returns to his dark room.

28. 一位禁欲者在死里逃生之后变成了一个花花公子。

29. 一位英俊小生杀死另外两位英俊小生只为他们三人长相一致。

30. 在黑暗的房间我装神弄鬼。真有一个傻瓜进门跪倒在我的面前。我一脚踹开他，继续我的享乐，另一个傻瓜就破门而入，举着菜刀来革我的命。

31. 在黑暗的房间，我打开收音机。我的自怜被收音机里话剧腔的爱情故事所唤醒。这时一个窃贼爬出我的床底，首先和我讨论人生的意义，然后向我发誓要重新做人。

32. 一个熟读《论语》的人把另一个熟读《论语》的人驳得体无完肤。

33. 杜甫得到了太多的赞誉，所以另一个杜甫肯定一无所获。

34. 在黑暗的房间，我奉承过一个死人。他不是我的祖先而是我的邻居。我为他编造出辉煌的一生，他铁青的脸上泛出红晕。多年以后，我在他孙子的家中饱餐一顿。

35. 在黑暗的房间，我虚构出一个女孩的肖像。一位友人说他认识这画上的女孩：她家住东城区春草胡同 35 号。我找到那里，她的邻居说她刚刚出了远门。

36. 兴冲冲的盗墓者面对已被盗掘一空的坟墓无事可干。

37. 无事可干的炊事员回到他黑暗的房间。

38/ In the dark room, a golden ring worn by three generations of my ancestors rolls off my finger onto the floor and cannot be found. That is why I suspect that below my room lies yet another dark room; that is why I suspect that all those who wear golden rings live below me.

39/ In the dark room, a bloke who has mistaken my door for another decides to make the best of his mistake. He takes off his backpack, washes his face, brushes his teeth, and then orders me to leave. I say that this is my home, that my life is rooted here, that I am going nowhere. Thereupon in the dark we start to wrestle.

Four: Of Dreary Good and Contentious Evil

40/ The smile on an ugly face may be less than refined, but can we still call it "good"? The falsetto may be pleasing to the ear, but is it "sincere"? Cui Yingying never fooled around or bantered in flirtation but she did commit the crime of adultery, the oil seller has a shiny red face but no girlfriend.

41/ The bird rises upwind, the boatman travels downstream. In their halls, in their graves, lords and ladies all do their duty, and servants and matchmakers all have their pleasure.

42/ And on both sides of the railroad, bandits await amnesty in exchange for submission; and in the capital, the heartless rich take precautions against bankruptcy.... Sometimes evil men are funny and make me double up with mirth. To avoid making fools of themselves, sometimes good men pretend to be fierce and malicious, and evil men are ashamed of evil deeds.

38. 在黑暗的房间，我祖传三代的金戒指滚落地面再也不见。我因此怀疑我房间的地下另有一个黑暗的房间；我因此怀疑每一个戴金戒指的人都住在我的下面。

39. 在黑暗的房间，一个走错了门的家伙将错就错。他放下背包，洗脸，刷牙，然后命令我离去。我说这是我的家，这是我的命根子，我哪儿也不去。于是我们在黑暗中扭打起来。

四、关于呆头呆脑的善与惹是生非的恶

40. 丑陋的面孔微笑，虽然欠雅，但是否可以称之为"善"？假嗓子唱歌，虽然动听，但是否"真诚"？崔莺莺从不打情骂俏却犯了通奸罪，卖油郎满面红光却没有女朋友。

41. 鸟儿逆风而起，舟子顺水而行。在厅堂，在基地，老爷、太太们各司其职，仆役、媒婆们各得其乐。

42. 而在铁路两旁，土匪们等待着受招安；而在京城，为富不仁者提防着破产……有时恶人们把我逗得前仰后合。为了免于出丑，有时善人们假装凶狠而恶人们羞于作恶。

43/ I undergo the destruction of the good, admiring the obesity of evil men in films, of a mind to share with them that doubtful privilege. Only for the chance of being trapped in the evil of a conspiracy do I return to my family, who cultivate the good, and impart to my family members the aesthetics of evil.

44/ You see, small-time thieves and pilferers will not destroy the world; and those who give in charity and have compassion do not demand the abolition of suffering.

45/ The good that meets the eye on every side: heavens, what mediocrity! And evil: it requires such inspiration!

46/ I declare that I am not of the cruel kind, although I do chase the meek rabbit and eat it. And surely the rabbit secretly makes up its mind to eat me in the next life, to satisfy its stomach, hungry for the good. It's just that its chance of success is uncertain, for in the next life, I plan to fly.

47/ One could, alone and lonely as one's shadow, travel a thousand miles, to avoid the sage's curse. The sage says: "Evil men like to live in groups". But among them, the principle of the good has been passed by vote: he who, alone and lonely as his shadow, travels a thousand miles is the one appearing to have a hidden intent.

48/ An old straw hat that lands on the head of a holy man turns into a holy thing, but even if a mosquito has drunk the blood of a holy man it must be killed. Pointing this out shows the contentiousness of evil (part 1).

49/ Evil men who give away their companions are charged with lesser evil, but good men who lavish praise upon their companions we must call more good than good. Pointing this out shows the contentiousness of evil (part 2).

50/ Oh, whose sword will I become to fight the opponent at close quarters? With whose iron spear will I clash, scattering sparks? And this sword of mine, whose fear will it be wields it, and whose joy?

43．我受到善的摧残，渴慕电影里恶人的肥胖，有心分享他们可疑的特权。只由于有可能陷入阴谋之恶，我才回到我修善的家庭，向我的家人传授恶的美学。

44．你看小偷小摸并不能毁灭世界；而施舍怜悯的人并不要求取消苦难。

45．这满目的善，天哪，多么平庸！而恶，多么需要灵感！

46．我声明我非残忍之辈，尽管我穷追那温顺的兔子并且吃掉它。而它一定曾暗下决心在来生吃掉我，以满足其向善之胃。只是它成功的希望渺茫，因为来生我准备飞翔。

47．或形只影单，独行千里，免于圣贤的诅咒。圣贤说："恶人喜群居。"而在他们中间，善的原则已被举手通过：是那形只影单、独行千里的人显得居心叵测。

48．一顶破草帽落在圣人头上就变成了圣物，而一只蚊子即便饮了圣人的血亦应被打死。指出这一点是恶在惹是生非之一。

49．恶人供出同伙，其罪恶便得以减免，而善人吹捧同伙，我们却必须说他是善上加善。指出这一点是恶在惹是生非之二。

50．啊，我将成为谁的钢刀与对手厮杀？我将遇上谁的铁矛碰出火花？而挥舞我这把钢刀的将是谁的恐惧、谁的欢乐？

51/ At one moment I walk around myself. You say: "This is impossible!"

52/ That is why I never proclaim my law and I merely call the court to order (Hammurabi did proclaim his law, so his kingdom perished), and that unproclaimed law of mine is lightning, it is flowers.

Five: Of My Intimate Experience of Things

53/ Thereupon I shun the towns, and shun all muddled thinking in the towns, in pursuit of the shadow cast by an eagle on this earth. Once I shun all muddled thinking, I understand that flames and floodwaves and beasts of prey are ruthless.

54/ Thereupon I gradually start to believe that there is an I inside this I, just like there is an eagle inside the eagle. Lightbulbs inside my body illuminate an entire society. When my flesh shakes, the sound of breaking crockery comes forth from my belly.

55/ After the river has made me a tribute of ripples the rock makes me a tribute of quartz crystals. Although they are not of the slightest use to me, I am grateful. In exchange, I make them a tribute of a song they do not need.

56/ Thereupon I shun my flesh, and turn into a drop of perfume, actually drowning an ant. Thereupon I turn into an ant, drilling my way into an elephant's brain, upsetting it so that it stamps all four of its legs. Thereupon I turn into an elephant, my entire body exuding a great stench. Thereupon I turn into a great stench, and those who cover their noses when they smell me are men. Thereupon I turn into a man, and a plaything of fate.

51. 有一瞬间我绕到自己的背后。你说："这不可能！"

52. 因此我从不公布我的法律，我只宣布开庭（汉谟拉比公布了他的法律，所以他的王国被消灭），而我那从不公布的法律就是雷电，就是花朵。

五、关于我对事物的亲密感受

53. 于是我避开市镇，避开那里的糊涂思想，追随一只鹰投在大地上的阴影。在我避开那些糊涂思想之后，我了解了火焰和洪水猛兽的无情。

54. 于是我渐渐相信，我中有我，正如鹰中有鹰。灯泡在我体内照亮一个社会。我的身体一摇晃，我的肚子里就传出碗碟摔碎的声响。

55. 在河水向我奉献波纹之后岩石向我奉献石英。虽然我拿它们毫无用处，但我感谢。作为回报，我向它们奉献它们并不需要的歌声。

56. 于是我避开我的肉体，变成一滴香水，竟然淹死一只蚂蚁。于是我变成一只蚂蚁，钻进大象的脑子，把它急得四脚直跺。于是我变成一头大象，浑身散发出臭味。于是我变成臭味，凡闻到我捂鼻子的就是人。于是我又变成一个人，被命运所戏弄。

57/ To love nature but leave its meaning aside, to love humankind but leave its integrity aside. Deep world: the deeper one's love for it, the heavier one's bias. This makes the ancestors howl with laughter. In unending changes they have walked around us and directly entered the homes of our posterity.

58/ Thereupon I turn into my posterity and let the rain test if I am waterproof. Thereupon I turn into rain, and splash upon the bald head of an intellectual. Thereupon I turn into that intellectual, detesting the world and its ways, pick up a stone from the ground and hurl it at the oppressor. Thereupon I turn into stone and oppressor at the same time: when I am hit by me, that sets both of my brains roaring.

59/ Silence. Only silence can attain symmetry with this raucous world.

60/ Hidden laws of this raucous world pass through the woman next door into my ear, grimly attacking my soft heart. So when dust soils my white gloves, I don't sue, I don't complain, but exert myself like an ox to imagine how well they wear on the hands of my soul, pure white.

61/ On rotting rice straw, seeking counsel from the face of the earth, my character becomes complete.

62/ Toward evening, I pull apart two fighting tramps: hence, with my head held high I enter mankind's friendship.

63/ Maybe in the end I will be enlightened, but before then compile a dictionary, so as to make men quickly speak out about all things, so as to make the intimate world find its place in language.

57．爱自然而悬置它的意义，爱人类而悬置他的德行。对一个纵深的世界，爱得越深，偏见越重。这令祖先们哈哈大笑。在无穷的变幻中，他们绕过我们，直接进了我们后代的家门。

58．于是我变成我的后代，让雨水检测我的防水性能。于是我变成雨水，淋在一个知识分子光秃的头顶。于是我变成这个知识分子，愤世嫉俗，从地上捡起一块石头投向压迫者。于是我同时变成石头和压迫者，在我被我击中的一刹那，我的两个脑子同时轰鸣。

59．沉默。只有沉默可以与喧闹的世界相对称。

60．喧闹世界的隐蔽的法则通过我的女邻居传入我的耳朵，冷酷打击我的温情。所以当尘土弄脏了我的白手套，我不起诉，不抱怨，而是像牛一样费力地想象它们怎样洁白地戴在我灵魂的手上。

61．在腐败的稻草上，以地貌为参照，我的性格完成。

62．傍晚，我拉开两个斗架的瘪三，我由此直着脖子进入人类的友谊。

63．也许我终将觉悟，而此前我将编定一部词典，以便人们将所有的事物快速说出，以便将亲密的世界安顿在语言中。

Six: Of Fighting, Tearing and Biting, and Death

64/ Well then, a sign that does not carry the weight of thinking, is that the eagle? But I have not yet turned into an eagle, but all foxes have turned into men. I need but feign to be an eagle, and a man will feign to be me. From the angle of poetry, our co-operation is seamless like a heavenly robe.

65/ I feign to be an eagle, but cannot feign its shyness; I feign to be an eagle, but have no way to fight and dive like the eagle. Even if at the very time of fighting, in its heart of hearts it is at a far remove from fighting, that is precisely why it is a costly bird; even if at the very time of fighting, its heart of hearts is calm, that is precisely why it borders well-nigh on the divine.

66/ It sweeps past the eaves of my dream: a word, a phantom. I do not like its pointed beak and sharp talons, but between the eagle and the earth remain regrettable understanding and brutal love.

67/ It flies on high, flying of itself, like its own shadow, restraining thunder in its heart. Like an ironed shirt it spreads its wings, and then it is the earth begins to fly.

68/ Legend has it that from the sky above the wilderness, eagle and snake fell fighting, and crushed Sophocles' head. Had they known who would be crushed, would they still have fought? Would they have let make-believe come true, and topped off this barbarian tragedy with the qualities of fate?

69/ In the eagle's eyes, three murdered hostages have returned to their teahouse; in the open wasteland, a movie is once again being shot; on the road connecting city and village, cattle once again let their odorless excrement and urine run freely, of misty poetic quality.

六、关于格斗、撕咬和死亡

64．那么，一个不承载思想的符号，是鹰吗？但我还没有变成过一只鹰，但所有的狐狸都变成了人。我把自己伪装成一只鹰，就有一个人伪装成我。从诗歌的角度看，我们合作得天衣无缝。

65．我伪装成一只鹰，但装不出它的羞涩；我伪装成一只鹰，但无法像鹰一样格斗和俯冲。即使在格斗时它也在内心远离格斗，因此它是昂贵的鸟；即使在俯冲时它也内心平静，因此它几乎接近于神性。

66．它从我梦的屋檐上掠过：一个字，一个幻像。我并不喜欢它的尖喙和利爪，但在它和大地之间保持着遗憾的理解和暴虐的爱情。

67．它高高飞翔，飞得那般自我，像自己的影子，把咆哮收敛在心中。像被熨过的一件衬衣，它展开翅膀，这时就是大地在飞动。

68．传说在旷野的天空，鹰蛇格斗掉下来，砸破了索福克勒斯的脑袋。要是它们知道谁将被砸死，它们是否还会格斗？它们是否会把死亡弄假成真，给野蛮的悲剧补上命运的特征？

69．在鹰眼里，三个被撕票的人回到了他们的茶馆；荒郊野外重又拍开了电影。在连接城市与村庄的道路上，牲口们重又把没有臭味的粪便泄得诗意朦胧。

70/ The eagle has the wisdom of blood, that is why it does not possess.

71/ In the end it is hunger that reminds it to fly, dive, tear and bite, like a hungry sun, a monk or his wrought-iron staff, like the eagle. In the end it is hunger that makes it too weak to fly, makes it into food for maggots, makes it into a two-meter-wide spread-eagled hide in the living room of a white-collared beauty.

72/ The body that the eagle destroys in space, it meets again in time.

73/ In the end it is death that does not distinguish mine and thine, high and low. That is not metaphysical death but death of the flesh: wounds festering, the body rigid. That is death of the flesh, and we partake in it.

74/ But we have always flattered and fawned on Death, so that instead, we can let the killer in our heart of hearts remain at large. The eagle understands this, that is why it never sheds a tear. It is we who shed tears. Otherwise, we mostly wear a smiling face—for whom?

75/ Between me and you flies the eagle, between thinking and life sleeps truth. That is why one should not be too quick to put eagle meat on the menu.

Seven: Of the Appearance of Truth

76/ It is too correct, all of it, so it is absurd; it is too absurd, all of it, so it is true. So let the correct be yet more correct, the absurd yet more absurd: such is the one and only way to make truth appear.

77/ So if I describe an eagle, it is in order to cut off its head; and if I do so, it is to seek evidence for ancient myth. Should it indeed have the strength to be reborn, the twentieth century will not have been without its miracles.

70. 鹰有血的智慧，因此从不占有。

71. 最终是饥饿提醒它飞翔、俯冲和撕咬，像饥饿的太阳、僧侣、镶铁禅杖，像鹰。最终是饥饿使它飞翔不动，成为苍蝇的食品，成为白领丽人小客厅里翼展两米的鹰皮。

72. 鹰在空间消灭的躯体，又在时间中与之相遇。

73. 最终是死亡，不分彼此，不分高下。那不是形而上之死而是肉体之死：伤口化脓，身体僵硬。那是肉体之死，我们参与其中。

74. 可我们对死神一向阿谀奉承，反倒让我们内心的杀手逍遥法外。鹰了解这一点，因此它从不落泪。落泪的是我们。此外，更多的时候我们还堆出笑脸——为谁？

75. 在我与你之间飞动着鹰，在思想和生命之间睡卧着真实。因此且慢将鹰肉列上菜谱。

七、关于真实的呈现

76. 太正确了，一切，所以荒谬；太荒谬了，一切，所以真实。所以让正确的更正确，让荒谬的更荒谬，乃是令真实呈现的不二法门。

77. 所以我描述出一只鹰，是为了砍下它的头；而我这样做，是要为古老的神话求取证明。倘若它果有再生之力，则当今世界并非没有奇迹发生。

78/ "This is impossible!" says the crow, "Why didn't I know I could be described as an eagle?" It hits its head against the wall: its head is still there, but with a hole in it.

79/ Calculate, force, tease, attack and praise: when thinking, all these measures for protecting oneself can occasionally be employed.

80/ So why don't you calculate your existence: that which your calculations will not yield is your soul. So why don't you force a poor man to swallow gold: let him have death and riches at the same time. So why don't you tease a mynah: should it then speak true words, do all you can to retain your composure.

81/ Early in the morning, a dog reports at my bed. As usual, I kick it fiercely, so as to make it yet more of a dog.

82/ In order to let a nitwit push his foolishness to the extreme, and in the end share a chariot with the sages, I try all possible ways to sing his praises. Once he has obtained irreplaceable pleasure from my praise, he declares that he is a nitwit, just like Socrates declared that he knew naught.

83/ Truth, a luxury word, a miserable word, a forced word with no choice: it is not in my dictionary.

84/ But it is in my word game. I play my word game until heaven and earth are upside down, could I really play it to make gods and devils cry at night? Or at least so that my reality of language is acceptable to ghosts?

85/ Ghosts are arrogant, and do not understand the way of the absurd. When my nose is squeezed and my mouth covered, and I wake with a shock on the edge of death, I acknowledge that the color red is red. Afterwards I put on my mask, a mask both pockmarked and wrinkled.

86/ It is too true! All of it, so it is correct; it is too correct, all of it, so it is absurd.

78. "这不可能！"乌鸦说，"我怎么不知道我可以被描述成一只鹰？"它在墙壁上撞击它的脑袋；它的脑袋还在，但却被撞出一个窟窿。

79. 计算、威逼、戏弄、打击和赞颂，这些用于自卫的手段在思想时可以偶然一用。

80. 所以你就计算一下你的存在吧，那计算不出的就是你的灵魂。所以你就威逼一个穷人吞下黄金吧，让他同时占有死亡和财富。所以你就戏弄一只八哥吧，倘若它说出真理你千万要冷静。

81. 清晨，一条狗到我的床前来报到。我照例狠狠踢它，以便它更是一条狗。

82. 为了让一个傻瓜将他的愚蠢推向极端，最终与那些圣贤不分轩轾，我想尽办法赞颂他。当他从我的赞颂中获得了不可替代的乐趣，他便宣布他是一个傻瓜，一如苏格拉底宣布他一无所知。

83. 真实，一个奢侈的词，一个悲惨的词，一个被逼无奈的词，不在我的词典中。

84. 但却在我的文字游戏里。我把文字游戏玩得天翻地覆，我真能玩到神鬼夜哭？或至少我给出的语言现实能让幽灵接受？

85. 幽灵是傲慢的，它们不理解荒谬之道。当我被捏住鼻子捂住嘴，从死亡的边缘一猛子醒来时，我承认，红色是红的，然后戴上我的面具，这面具上既有麻子也有皱纹。

86. 太真实了！一切，所以正确；太正确了，一切，所以荒谬。

87/ If you are tired of truth, then on top of your mask wear a pair of sunglasses. All you need to do is whisper this one sentence: "Truth will not save us."

Eight: Of My Meaningless Life

88/ Among men there are men who are no men, just like among eagles there are eagles that are no eagles: there are eagles that are forced to pace up and down the alleyways, and there are men who are forced to fly through the air.

89/ When dusk is deep I go to sleep, come morning light I end my night. I always first dream of doctors with a fever and mailmen with a toothache, and then meet them: so in order to meet myself, I must first dream of myself, but to dream of oneself is really embarrassing.

90/ One time, I dreamt of a blind man who queried me about so-and-so. I replied that I had heard of so-and-so but did not know him. When I woke, I hollered with astonishment: I was the one the blind man wanted!

91/ Only when a nail is stuck in my hand does truth emerge from my hand; only when a cloud of black smoke chokes me so that tears run down my cheeks do I experience my existence. Ten straight-backed fairies riding one white horse tear my heart asunder.

92/ That is why I change my name, hide my identity, float with the clouds to the four winds and submit to the will of heaven.

93/ I once demanded of the proprietress of a small inn that she make me the proprietor of that small inn. While she was caught in utter amazement I further demanded that she offer me board and lodging free of charge. She asked me: "Who are you? Where do you come from?" I said: "I am the one with two demands. Take your pick."

87. 如果你已厌倦了真实，你就在你的面具上再戴一副墨镜吧。你只需小声嘀咕一句："真实并不能将我们拯救。"

八、关于我的无意义的生活

88. 在人群里有的人不是人，就像在鹰群里有的鹰不是鹰；有的鹰被迫在胡同里徘徊，有的人被迫飞翔在空中。

89. 天一黑我就入睡，天一亮我就起床。我总是首先梦见发烧的医生、牙疼的邮递员，然后遇见他们；所以为了遇见自己，我必须首先将自己梦见，而梦见自己的确使人难为情。

90. 有一次，我梦见一个瞎子向我打听某某。我回答我听说过此人但是并不认识。待我醒来，我惊异得嗷嗷大叫：我就是那瞎子要找的人！

91. 只有当一根钉子扎到我的手上，我的手才显现出真实；只有当一阵黑烟呛得我流泪，我才感受到我的存在。一匹白马上端骑着的十位仙女撕碎了我的心。

92. 为此我改名换姓，隐瞒起身份，云游四方，听天由命。

93. 我曾向一家小客店的老板娘要求做这家小客店的老板。在她惊讶不已之际我又向她要求免费供应我食宿。她问我："你是谁？你从哪里来？"我说："我就是这提出两项要求的人。你选择吧。"

94/ I once got lost in a gloomy mansion, like an assassin disturbing the order of things, like an evil man raising fear among the girls. Right then, I tasted another way of getting lost: lost in glee—and thus forgot my chaos and my fear.

95/ I once got stuck in a city under siege, and ran into an aged scholar. When I pointed out my "plight" and "loneliness" to him, he said he was concerned only with the blessedness of all men under heaven. So I spat my phlegm into the crow's beak.

96/ I once queried an official about the key to officialdom, and he urged me to go home and be a good citizen. I asked him: "Do you want to know how to turn stone to gold?" When a greedy look lit up his eyes, I said: "I'll keep my secret too."

97/ If you can sit down, then sit down; if you can lie down, then lie down. To make a bare living, every day I do more than three kinds of work. But whenever I finish one of them, there is a man who collects the reward that is due to me.

98/ The sage says: "The eagle revels in its soaring." Wrong, the eagle does not revel in its soaring, any more than man revels in his walking.

99/ So please allow me to stay in your house for an hour, because an eagle plans to reside in a chamber of my heart for a week. If you accept me, I will gladly turn into the image you hope for, but not for too long, or my true features will be thoroughly laid bare.

Translated by Maghiel van Crevel

94. 我曾迷失在一座阴森的府宅，像一名刺客搅乱了那里的秩序，像一个恶棍激发出小姐们的恐惧。这时我品尝到另一种迷失——迷失于快乐，我因而忘记了自己的混乱和恐惧。

95. 我曾身陷一座被围困的城市，我曾遇到过一位年迈的书生。当我向他指出我们的"处境"和"孤独"，他说他只关心天下人的福祉。所以我是把一口痰吐进了乌鸦的嘴里。

96. 我曾向一个官吏打听升官的窍门，他劝我回家去做一个好公民。我问他："你是否想知道怎样把石头点化成黄金？"当他露出贪婪的目光，我说："我也保密。"

97. 能坐下就坐下，能躺下就躺下。为了活命，我每天干三种以上的工作。但每当我干完一份工作，总有一个人领走我应得的报酬。

98. 圣贤说："鹰陶醉于翱翔。"不对，鹰并不陶醉于翱翔，就像人并不陶醉于行走。

99. 所以请允许我在你的房间待上一小时，因为一只鹰打算在我的心室里居住一星期。如果你接受我，我乐于变成你所希望的形象，但时间不能太久，否则我的本相就会暴露无遗。

1997.10—1998.4
新德里—北京

CLOSE SHOTS AND DISTANT VIEWS

Birds

Birds are the highest creatures we can see with our naked eyes. Now and then, they sing, curse, fall into silence. We know nothing about the sky above them: that is the realm of irrationality or of huge nihilism. Thus birds create the boundary of our rationality and the fulcrum of cosmic order. It is said that birds can behold the sun: whereas we will feel dizzy in one second, and six seconds later go blind. According to mythology, Zeus presented himself as a swan to fuck Leda; God occupied Mary in the semblance of a dove. There is a line from the Book of Songs: "Heaven let its black bird descend, and the Shang dynasty thus came into being." Although some experts argue that this black bird is nothing but the penis, still let's forget it. Coming to own the world as a bird is a god's privilege; as is an emperor's disguising himself as attendant to pay a private visit. Hence we may say, God is used to condescending. Hence birds are the mediators between earth and heaven, counters between man and God; and the stairs, passageways, that form quasi-deities. Duckbills copy the appearance of birds; bats fly in a birdlike way; and clumsy fowls could be called "degenerate angels." The birds we are singing for – their gorgeous feathers, their light bones – are half-birds: mysterious creatures, seeds in metaphysics.

近景和远景

鸟

鸟是我们凭肉眼所能望见的最高处的生物，有时歌唱，有时诅咒，有时沉默。对于鸟之上的天空，我们一无所知：那里是非理性的王国，巨大无边的虚无；因此鸟是我们理性的边界，是宇宙秩序的支点。据说鸟能望日，至少鹰，作为鸟类之王，能够做到这一点；而假如我们斗胆窥日，一秒钟之后我们便会头晕目眩，六秒钟之后我们便会双目失明。传说宙斯化作一只天鹅与丽达成欢，上帝化作一只鸽子与玛丽亚交配。《诗经》上说："天命玄鸟，降而生商。"尽管有人指出：玄鸟者，鸡巴也，但咱们或可不信。自降为鸟是上帝占有世界的手段，有似人间帝王为微服私访，须扮作他的仆人。因此上帝习惯于屈尊。因此鸟是大地与天空的中介，是横隔在人神之间的桌子，是阶梯，是通道，是半神。鸭嘴兽模仿鸟的外观，蝙蝠模仿鸟的飞翔，而笨重的家禽则堪称"堕落的天使"。我们所歌唱的鸟——它绚丽的羽毛，它轻盈的骨骼——仅仅是鸟的一半。鸟：神秘的生物，形而上的种籽。

Fire

Fire cannot illuminate fire; what is illuminated by fire is not fire. Fire illuminated Troy, fire illuminated Emperor Qin Shi's face; fire illuminated the crucible of the alchemist, fire illuminated leaders and masses. All these fires are one fire – element, passion – predating logic. Zoroaster only gets it half right: fire has to do with the bright and clean, as opposed to the dark and foul. But he neglects the fact that fire is born of darkness, mistakenly opposing fire to death. Because fire is pure, it is faced with death; because fire is exclusive, it tends to be viewed as cold-blooded and evil. People usually see fire as the spirit of creation, not knowing it is also the spirit of destruction. Fire is free, paternal and holy: without form, without mass, it neither spurs the growth of any life, nor supports any standing object. Just as those full of ambition must give up hope, those who accept fire must accept great sacrifice.

火焰

火焰不能照亮火焰，被火焰照亮的不是火焰. 火焰照亮特洛伊城，火焰照亮秦始皇的面孔，火焰照亮炼金术士的坩埚，火焰照亮革命的领袖和群众。这所有的火焰是一个火焰——元素，激情——先于逻辑而存在。琐罗亚斯德说对了一半：火焰与光明、洁净有关，对立于黑暗与恶浊。但他忽视了火焰诞生于黑暗的事实，而且错误地将火焰与死亡对立起来。由于火焰是纯洁的，因而面临着死亡；由于火焰具有排他性，因而倾向于冷酷和邪恶。人们通常视火焰为创造的精灵，殊不知火焰也是毁灭的精灵。自由的、父性的、神圣的火焰，无形式、无质量的火焰，不能促使任何生物生长，不能支撑任何物体站立。就像满怀理想的人必须放弃希望，接受火焰的人必须接受伟大的牺牲。

Shadow

As I grow up, I begin to have a shadow. I cannot ignore it, unless it merges into another, greater shadow – night. But whose shadow is night? The earth casts its shadow on the moon, hence the lunar eclipse: the moon casts its shadow on the earth, hence the solar eclipse. All of us live in shadow. On the other side of the shadow lies fire; and shadow gives us our only basis for measuring the sun. In daily life, because there is only one sun, nothing can have multiple shadows; as for our souls, the shadow is the sum total of desire, selfishness, fear, vanity, jealousy, cruelty and death. Shadow endows things with reality. To strip a thing of its reality, one only needs to strip it of its shadow. The sea has no shadow; therefore it feels like an illusion. Objects in our dreams have no shadow; therefore they form another world. Thus people have every reason to believe that ghosts have no shadow.

阴影

我长大成人，我有了阴影。我对它不可能视而不见，除非它融入更大的阴影——黑夜；而黑夜是什么人或什么东西的阴影呢？地球投影于月球是为月食；月球投影于地球是为日食。所有的人都生活在阴影之中。阴影的反面是火焰。阴影是我们测算太阳的唯一依凭。在我们的日常生活范围内，由于太阳只有一个，因而任何一件物体都不可能有多重阴影；而对我们的灵魂来说，阴影就是欲望、私心、恐惧、虚荣、嫉妒、残忍和死亡的总和。是阴影赋予事物真实性。剥夺一件事物的真实性只需拿去它的阴影。海洋没有阴影，因而使我们感到虚幻；我们梦中的物体没有阴影，因而它们构成了另一个世界。人们由此合情合理地认定鬼魂是没有阴影的。

I

Animals are superstitious, plants have thoughts, god has defects, human beings have souls. The so-called "human soul" namely refers to his "inner self." People have an "outer self" life: to keep out hardships, fight back, work, shake hands, pat shoulders, even lie and cheat. But to a certain extend people's "inner self" is always composed, life always pours into its intended direction. It's not that the "outer self" is the "inner self's" mask, it's more that the "outer self's" rules are not suitable for the "inner self." If you nearly touch or harm one's "outer self," then you don't have any effect or disturb him; however in case you deepen to his "inner self," then his attitude will completely change. Fate, suffering, love and death all those concepts that only have meaning for the "inner self," this is what we know as the "secret of the soul". Jung called the blind instinct, which guided him his "feminine tendencies," in fact it was his "inner self." This is the fragile I; wrapped layers after layers, carefully protected, hidden, and related to infinity.

我

动物是有迷信的，植物是有思想的，神是有缺陷的，人是有灵魂的。所谓"人的灵魂"，即指他"内在的我"。人们用"外在的我"生活：抵挡风雨，打架斗殴，工作，握手，拍肩膀，甚至撒谎骗人。但在一定程度上，人们"内在的我"始终镇定自若，生命始终向着其既定的方向涌进。这不是说"外在的我"是"内在的我"的面具，而是说"外在的我"的法则不适于"内在的我"。若你仅触及或伤害到一个人"外在的我"，则你对他还不能构成影响和打扰；而一旦你深入到他"内在的我"，则他的精神面貌将彻底改变。命运、痛苦、爱和死亡都只对"内在的我"拥有意义。所谓"灵魂的秘密"正在于此。荣格曾经把他身上那起着指导作用的、盲目的直觉称作他的"女性倾向"，他所说的实际上就是他"内在的我"。这是被层层包裹，小心保护、隐蔽的，脆弱的我，与无限有关。

Peony

Mu-dan, the peony, is a flower of hedonism: it differs from the rose which has a double nature, flesh and spirit; whereas the peony has only flesh, just as the chrysanthemum has only spirit. Because of this, the peony doesn't exist before it blossoms or after it fades away. Liu Yuxi's line: "The peony is the only national beauty that gives sensation when it opens." It is the sort of plant that can hardly be redeemed, its fleshy glamour hardly rejected. Those of aristocratic families love its secular beauty, whereas ordinary people enjoy its exuberance. In the novel The Lost Voice of the White Snow it is said "the peony flower represents property during springtime." Along with this sentence is also: "being pricked by an emerald hairpin, the peony blossom becomes more beautiful." Obviously, the peony here must be taken as symbol of female genitalia. Peony, mu-dan, means male; dan in the ancient syntax was a mined red stone. Etymologically, mu-dan, the peony, is a male flower. Its sexual genre was changed purely because of its natural suggestiveness. In order to enforce the identity of "king of flowers" upon the peony, and to inject spirit into its flesh, someone invented the story that Empress Wu Zetian once ordered all flowers growing in the Upper Garden of Chang'an City to be forced to blossom in winter, and the peony was later banished and exiled to the city of Luoyang for its disobedience. It's a pity that the peony didn't change into a rose under the magic of this legend. It is the nature of the peony to despise the rose. It seems a flower that would be part of the Renaissance, but actually was not.

牡丹

牡丹是享乐主义之花。它不像玫瑰具有肉体和精神两重性，它只有肉体，就像菊花只有精神。正因为如此，牡丹在开花之前和凋谢之后根本就不存在。刘禹锡诗云："唯有牡丹真国色，花开时节动京城。"这是一种不得超升的植物，其肉体的魅力难于为人们的肉体所拒绝：富家子弟一向爱其俗丽，平头百姓一向爱其丰腴。是故《白雪遗音》有"牡丹花儿春富贵"之句。此外，该书又有"玉簪轻刺牡丹开"之辞。这显然是以牡丹象征女性性器。牡丹本为雄性之花，它之所以被改换性别，纯粹出于其自然暗示。为了使牡丹更加符合其"花中之王"的身份，为了向牡丹灌注精神因素，有人特传武则天尝命上苑百花于冬令开放，唯牡丹抗旨不从，被贬东都。可惜牡丹并未受此传奇魔法而摇身一变为玫瑰。牡丹鄙视玫瑰，此其天性。它貌似文艺复兴所需要的花朵，其实不然。

Poison

Things poisonous are beautiful and dangerous. We may transpose this sentence into, beautiful and dangerous things are poisonous. Both sentences consequently produce the concept of beauty/snake. Usually poisonous things themselves are not evil: datura, oleander, cobra, are parts of nature, but since their toxin has been extracted by pharmacists, some bad eggs succeed in realizing conspiracies and some good eggs succeed in dying. Let alone the practical use of poison – it usually divides people into poison throwers and victims, or people in front of the curtain and the ones behind it. It also prods politicians with a stick evolved from fairy tales. As a result, murder cases take on aesthetic meanings. Poison takes a skull as its token. It has the potential to change the environment and human psychology: a room with poison deposited in it is different from other rooms; and a man who has poison in his pocket could be either a devil or an accomplice. As for those who commit suicide with poison, I almost have nothing to say except for one thing: that is, before they take poison, each of them has flawed, becoming transformed into two persons. One has become a poison thrower at oneself. Thus we may say that all suicides committed by means of taking poison are essentially conspiratorial.

毒药

有毒的事物是美丽而危险的。这句话也可以反过来说，即美丽而危险的事物是有毒的。美女蛇便是这种观念的产物。按说有毒的事物本身并不是罪恶：曼陀罗、夹竹桃、眼镜蛇等，同样是大自然的组成部分；只是它们的毒素被药剂师提取，于是一些人阴谋得逞，另一些人死于非命。撇开毒药的实际应用不谈——毒药通常把人区分为投毒者和受害者、幕前的人和幕后的人；同时它又把政治和童话粘连在一起，赋予毒杀以某种审美意义。毒药以骷髅为形象；它有着改变环境和人类心理的巨大能量：一间存放毒药的房屋不再等同于一般房屋，而怀揣毒药的人不是恶魔就是帮凶。至于服毒自杀者，我没什么可说的。唯一可以说明的一点是，每一个自杀者在服毒之前都分裂为两人。他给自己下毒。因此凡服毒自杀都带有阴谋的性质。

Silver

Do you know silver has been humiliated? It was unimaginable that it would be used for purchase, investment, compensation and gambling. People humiliate it by underestimating its value, as if it were not a touchable moon, the solidity of waves, the roof of our dreams or a village for us to feel nostalgia within. Ancient Egyptians were more clever than we when they showed their respect for silver. During the years between 1780-1580 B.C., Egyptian law stipulated that silver was two times more valuable than gold. But it doesn't mean that silver was not humiliated by being treated like this. The fact is that silver has nothing to do with gold. If we say that gold is hot with hubbub, then silver is cool with silence. There are blood relations between silver and copper and iron. In Sanskrit, the word "silver" means "brightness," so when people humiliate silver, they do the same to all bright things. Silver is healthful because it is good at killing germs; silver is generous because it functions to conduct electricity. Yet it has been humiliated. People do not understand it at all; and silver in its loneliness fells shy about sighing with the interjection: oh!

银子

人们污辱了银子。银子从没想到人们会用银子来购买、投资、赔偿和赌博。人们污辱了银子，一再贬低银子的价值，好像银子不是我们的怀旧之乡，不是我们梦的屋顶、固体的波浪、可触摸的月亮。古埃及人稍微懂得尊重银子：大约在公元前 1780—公元前1580 年间，埃及王朝的法典中规定，银价是金价的两倍。但古埃及人依然污辱了银子，因为银子与黄金无关：如果说黄金是西方的金属，那么银子便是东方的金属；如果说黄金是喧嚣而灼热的，那么银子便是寂静而沁凉的，它只与铜和铁有血缘之亲。在梵文中，银子一词的原意为"明亮"，因此人们污辱银子，也就是污辱一切明亮的东西。由于银子有杀菌力，因此银子是健康的；由于银子具有高强的导电功能，因此银子是慷慨的。但人们污辱了银子，人们根本不理解它。它孤独而羞涩，不好意思发出感慨：哦，孤独的银子！

City

Here is the rising of a city: at the beginning there is trade; there are people exchanging salt, leather, grain and luxury goods. Those who came from distant places set up the first block of shanties; then more shanties with streets, cellars, squares, toilets and sewers between and under them. Some find work for themselves right there, in manufacturing and processing. When dusk comes, restaurants and brothels shoot up out of man's desire for entertainment. This results in city-civilization. The rise of cities is different from that of villages: people inhabiting one village usually come from one family, regarding the father as king (sometimes a certain village may develop into a "city," but actually it is a village enlarged). But a real city is a choice freely made by man and woman, originating from different families and tribes. A mixed inheritance brings ideas and virtues which divide into schools later; the same brings crime and conflict which require courts of justice and jails. People have to compromise to preserve their existence as a whole. Then one day, a stranger arrives. He sets down his small valise, walks from the inn to the square blowing a bugle, and proclaims to the baffled audience that he has come to be the head of the city as per heaven's intention; and people should show respect, protect him and pay him taxes.

城市

城市的兴起是这样的：起初是贸易。在天然的十字路口，起初是交换食盐、兽皮、粮食和奢侈品的人们，其中远道而来的人们搭起最初的窝棚。随后窝棚多起米，有了街道、地窖、广场、厕所和下水道。有人就地展开制造业、加工业。黄昏来临，在人们对娱乐的需求中，酒馆和妓院拔地而起。于是有了最初的城市文明。城市的兴起不同于村庄的兴起：居住在同一村庄里的人往往属于同一家族，以父亲为君主 (有时某个村庄也能发展为 "城市"，但说到底，那是一个放大了的村庄)；而真正的城市却是来自不同家族、部落的男女自由选择的杂居之地。杂居孕育了思想和善，于是有了学校；杂居孕育了罪恶和冲突，于是有了法庭和监狱。人们不得不达成妥协，以维护整体的生存。终于有一天，一个陌生人来到城市。他放下少许的行李，吹着喇叭，从客栈走到广场，向莫名其妙的居民宣布：他秉承天意来做这城市的首领；人们必须尊敬他，保护他，并向他纳税。

Cards

The essence of inventing a game is to invent a set of rules and to leave room for contingency in which to entertain the players. So far as playing cards is concerned, people actually play with the unknown, according to the rules. They are mysterious, the diamonds, hearts, spades and clover, and it is impossible that they stand for nothing. I guess those figures, the Caesar, Charlemagne, Alexander the Great, King David, Jacob's wife Rachel and the heroine Judith, do want to say something to the players. Each time when cards are shuffled again, history is again fabricated; and who dares to say that history is not a made-up story? Constant changes take place during the process of fabrication. Thus cards are also obtained to practice divination. Intellectuals take card-playing as the lowest game among games of intelligence, since it requires little intelligence and good luck is far more important. There are times when you win; your opponents do not praise the good work you have done, but the good luck you seem to have. That they are not convinced makes you unsatisfied. So you play again, and this time you might fall into the trough from the wave's crest. Isn't it the cards' entertaining themselves by making vengeful mockery of the players?

扑克牌

发明一种游戏，也便同时发明了一种偶然性和一套规则；偶然性在规则中时隐时现，便把欢娱之情带给游戏者。具体说到打牌，人们是按照规则玩着不可知：扑克牌上那些方块、那些红桃、那些梅花、那些黑桃，或许真有某些神秘的暗示，而恺撒大帝、查理大帝、亚历山大大帝、大卫王，以及雅各之妻拉结、女勇士朱迪斯等人，或许真有什么话要对玩牌的人讲。扑克牌每重新排列组合一次，历史便被重新虚构一回，但谁又能肯定地说历史不是虚构的产物呢？在虚构中，变化是无穷的，因此扑克牌也被用来占卜。有人认为打牌是所有智力游戏中最低级的一种，因为它只需要那么一点点智力，更多的是靠运气。有时你赢了牌，别人不夸你牌打得好，而夸你的牌运好——这是他们不服气，弄得你也不舒服，于是再打一把。但或许这一次你就真的从最高峰跌到了最低谷。所以谁能说扑克牌对于智力不是怀着报复性的嘲讽呢？

Bicycle

The mechanism of a bicycle works in a simple way, but it is not inferior to any other advanced means of transportation in displaying the beauty of mathematics and physics. Its roller chain and cranks have become plundered possibilities through people making brand-new designs built upon bicycles and resorting to other principles. This is nothing but the fulfillment of an idea. We are ready to take it as a lively body with a soul in it, since it is fatally connected with our view of the world, and even defines our way of living. It reminds us of some interesting figures, like the late-Qing dynasty prostitute Sai Jinhua, and the socialist hero Lei Feng. The developing level of our social economy, culture and political system is marked by the bicycle. Explanations of the word "bicycle" in dictionaries should be enlarged by adding self-reliance, self-transportation. Two wheels and a framework might compose another machine, yet the bicycle coalesces our random thoughts: sometimes when I am riding my shabby bike down the crowded street, I feel I am going to take off – with everyone watching – into the azure of the sky, if I speed up a little bit.

自行车

尽管自行车是一种简单机械，但它在体现数学之美和物理学之美等方面，却绝不亚于其他更先进的交通工具。它的曲柄和链条传动装置封死了人们再依据其他原理设想全新自行车的可能性。任何事物的完满不过如此。由于自行车的完满，由于它和我们生活的密切联系——甚至可以说它规定了我们的生活方式——我们几乎要把它看成一个有灵魂的生命体。……它是我们这个社会经济、文化、政治水平的标志。词典中"自行车"一词的含义应该扩大。应该加上"自行车意味着自力更生、自己运送自己"的象征含义。它又不仅仅是两个轮子、一副钢架，它帮助我们遐想：在嘈杂拥挤的大街上，时常，我骑着我破旧的自行车，感觉自己就要飞升——在众目睽睽之下骑上蓝天——如果我骑得再快一点！

Wind

The only lifeless movement on the earth, thus an eternal movement, is the wind. Strictly speaking, we can not see it; what we see is the floating dust, the turbulent clouds and the waving leaves. Although walking against the wind has nothing to do with evading death, walking with the wind does make us feel that life is something great. When we stop and stand in the wind, we can hear it skimming past our ears and come to believe in the existence of an objective world; but Buddhists that it is because of the movement of our hearts. Our hearts move always; but why is it that sometimes we cannot hear the wind? Between gusts of wind, the earth is silent, as if plants have ceased to grow and time has been killed. Only when the wind rises again, life glitters again. So it is reasonable to say that it is the wind that promotes life. Paul Valery said, "The wind is rising: you must try to live!" Alas, wind, windfall, windbreaker, windmill, wind furnace, wind vane ... all those have things to do with the wind, also with us. But we are not the wind. Yet even without life, the wind ought to blow until the last day, if there is such a day.

风

大地上唯一一种没有生命的运动——因而是永恒的运动——是风。严格地说我们看不见风;我们看到的是灰沙在飞舞、白云在翻滚、树叶在扇动。尽管逆风而行并不等同于逆死亡而行,但当我们顺风而行时,我们有时的确觉得活着是一件惬意的事;而在风中伫立片刻,我们就能听到风声。风从我们耳边掠过,那是实实在在的客观宇宙之流变。可佛家偏说那是我们的心在动。难道我们的心不是一直在动吗?可为什么有时我们又听不到风声?在风与风之间,大地一片寂静,仿佛植物不再生长,仿佛时间流到了尽头。只有当风再一次刮起,生命才重新闪耀。所以说是风推动了生命,带动了生命。瓦雷里说:"起风了,只有试着活下去这一条路。"啊,风,风声,风琴,风衣,风车,风向标,风信子……一切与风有关的事物都与我们有关。可风不是我们,风超越生命。无生命的风将会刮到最后一日,如果真有这一日的话。

Ghosts

Death is a private affair for the dead. It is the same thing for the living when it acts upon one through ghosts. I am not talking in the vein of metaphor-usage: it's an old idea that without ghosts the concept of death would be void. Then, will we be lucky enough to witness apparitions? Will ghosts die? If I turn out to be a ghost, will animals experience their transformations? I can hardly imagine that ghosts would like to be quiet, sit for ten minutes or have a sleep. That we are afraid of ghosts means childhood has been prolonged in our bodies. What makes us uneasy is not the evil of ghosts (perhaps most of them are kind). It's the unknown that frustrates us. We don't feel fearful of ancient ghosts (Xiang Yu or Caesar). The dreadful ghosts compose a portion of our lives. Anthropologists say that the total population of humans who have gone is 79 billion, which could be interpreted as our sharing the world with 79 billion ghosts. If there were no ghosts then heaven and hell would be abolished; and logically good people wouldn't be comforted and bad ones would go unpunished. It's vulgar and unintellectual to say so, but we are afraid that we will be disappointed by disappointing ghosts.

幽灵

死亡纯属死者的个人私事。死亡通过幽灵作用于生者，也纯属生者的个人私事。我不是以比喻的口吻来谈论幽灵，我谈论的是一个古老的观念：没有幽灵，死亡便是空洞的。那么幽灵会出现吗？幽灵会死亡吗？如果我死后会变成幽灵，动物也能变成幽灵吗？很难想象幽灵能够安静下来，坐十分钟，或睡上一觉。对于幽灵的恐惧标志着童年在我们身上的延续。我们并不是恐惧幽灵之恶（或许大多数幽灵是善的），我们恐惧的是未知数；我们也并不恐惧古老的幽灵（比如恺撒或项羽），我们所恐惧的幽灵是我们生存的一部分。据说古往今来世界总人口达 790 亿，这就是说我们也许在与 790 亿个幽灵共用一个世界。而如果没有幽灵就没有天堂和地狱；如果没有天堂和地狱，好人就得不到安慰，坏人就得不到惩罚。这样说既庸俗又不智。但我们真怕因为令幽灵大失所望而弄得我们自己大失所望。

Ruins

Eulogizing the sublime form of a ruin is the same as eulogizing an atrocity, and looking with indifference at that lofty form is the same as admitting that we lack the ability to be affected by it. The reason we have these two difficult states of mind when facing a ruin is that a ruin's existence is vastly greater than ours; between us and ruins there is practically no proportion to speak of. Yet, even if we acknowledge our insignificance, ruins still refuse to act as people and receive us: a ruin is the home of phantoms, only they are qualified to loiter there, so it changes all who enter into ghosts. A ruin is not the same as a construction site: it has won the perfection and honor that things yet to be completed anticipate. Its stones that once stood are far more costly than stones that never stood; they collapse but in our minds are prepared whensoever to stand again. Times has weight; history comes at a cost. Ruins are the combining of roofs and the ground into one, ever taller green grass covers the traces of fire, the marks of sunshine and rainfall. Amid silent ruins, only the stone columns stand apart, talking to themselves – that is the nature of a building, the essence of creation, the nature of the spirit of mankind.

废墟

赞美废墟的崇高形态等于赞美暴行，而漠视废墟的崇高形态等于承认我们缺乏感受力。面对废墟我们之所以有此两难心态，乃是由于废墟的存在远远大于我们的存在，在我们与废墟之间几乎没有比例可言。不过，即使我们承认自己渺小，废墟依然拒绝作为人将我们接纳：废墟是幽灵之家，只有幽灵才有资格徜徉其间，因此它把每一位进入者都变成幽灵。废墟不同于建筑工地：它达到过未完成的事物所期待的光荣和完美，它那些站立过的石头比从未站立过的石头要昂贵得多，它们倒塌了但随时准备在我们的脑海中重新站立。时间是有重量的，历史是有代价的。废墟是屋顶与大地的合二为一，越长越高的青草遮掩了那火烧的痕迹、日晒雨淋的痕迹。在寂静的废墟间，茕茕孑立、自言自语的只有柱石，那是建筑的本质、创造的本质、人类精神的本质。

Mirage

The refraction of sun-rays in air constructs a mirage, which could be taken as the best example to explain the way in which matter turns into spirit: look at spiritual houses, spiritual squares, spiritual wild lilies, one hundred and eight heroes from the Water Margins, thirty-six girlfriends of Jia Baoyu, etc. That's another kind of life, like something we occasionally recall, like a lonely city standing at the end of the road which we occasionally see. The mirage – another way to put it is the castle in the air – ignores laws and rules of the secular world, and drives people to the position of waiting to be selected. It belongs neither to the present nor to the past, nor to the future. Being a metaphor of our homeland and Utopia, it is disassociated from time. Its theological meaning: God has no bed in heaven. Its philosophical meaning: a blink is eternity. Its aesthetic meaning: only qualified persons are allowed to appreciate such distancing. Its ethical meaning: to pay close attention to the word "happiness" in your dejections and hesitations; that is happiness. A mirage is suggested by all pictures, poems and books. If you have never seen any mirage, you may imagine it via the rainbow.

Translated by Inara Cedrins, Sarah Anais Aubry and the author

海市蜃楼

大气中由于光线的折射作用而形成海市蜃楼。那是物质变精神的最好例证：看那精神的房屋、精神的广场、精神的野百合、一百零八条好汉、贾宝玉的三十六个女朋友，等等等等。那是另一种生活，好似一段往事被我们偶然忆及，好似大路尽头一座孤城被我们偶然望见。海市蜃楼——换一种说法：空中楼阁——置世俗律令于不顾，置人类于被挑选的境地。它既不属于现在，也不属于过去，也不属于未来。作为我们关于家园和乌托邦的隐喻，它游离于时间之外。其神学意义在于：上帝不在天堂；其哲学意义在于：瞬间即成永恒；其美学意义在于：远方是一种境界；其伦理学意义在于：幸福即是在苦闷彷徨中对于幸福的关注。任何一幅画、一首诗、一本书，都与海市蜃楼有关。你若不曾见过海市蜃楼，你可以通过彩虹来想象。

1992—1994

MISFORTUNE (Excerp)

A 00000

He never looks back, yet knows I am lurking.

He shouts: "Stop on the edge of cliff, or your body won't withstand the anger."

He turns, sees the purple aura rising above me. He shakes his head, and the sun sinks into the trees.

He sees the devil's shadow behind me. (He must have witnessed Almond's smile, heard the azaleas sing.)

August, you must avoid crows. You must wake up early in September. You'll have great future, he predicts, but mean spirits will block your path.

Another man appears in the lane and the stranger vanishes. I fidget. Could he be my fate?

We pass, brush shoulders; he'll catch me again in this maze of ruins.

A crow flies across August's forehead.

I close my eyes, and the crow sings, "Don't be afraid. Your body is not yours, it is a hotel for others."

厄运 （节选）

A 00000

两个人的小巷，他不曾回头却知道我走在他的身后。

他喝斥，他背诵："必须悬崖勒马，你脆弱的身体承担不了愤怒。"

他转过身来，一眼就看到我的头顶有紫气在上升。他摇一摇头，太阳快速移向树后。

他说他看到了我身后的鬼影。（这样的人，肯定目睹过巴旦杏的微笑，肯定听得见杜鹃花的歌声。）

"八月，你要躲避乌鸦。九月，你得天天早起。"

他预言我将有远大前程，但眼下正为小人所诟病。

小巷里出现了第三个人，我面前的陌生人随即杳无踪影。我忐忑不安，猜想那迎面走来的就是我的命运。

我和我的命运擦肩而过；

在这座衰败的迷宫中他终究会再次跟上我。

一只乌鸦掠过我八月的额头。我闭眼，但听得乌鸦说道："别害怕，你并非你自己，使用着你身体的是众多个生命。"

B 00007 (identity unclear)

The shrewd woman chokes under the telephone pole,

Fiery ears underground catch her words.

A man shaving in the cave cuts himself.

The vanished trudge below.

Under the searchlight my spirit finds secrets—orange bodies of the missing.

He climbs the wall, peeks at the flowers and falls when they scream.

Has he returned to his childhood, is this death or eternity?

Wandering, wind and rain in the distance, he bumps into a friend who owes him money, a panicked smile on his face.

Hungry, they embrace, refusing to talk business.

Past the opera house, past the laundry, they sneak into a banquet like plainclothes, searching for a basement bathroom.

Three cops arrest them, eighteen women accuse them of obscenities.

The debtor reaches for a fake pass but pulls out a jar of Tiger Balm.

"Please accept this humble gift," he says. But they blindfold him, take him to jail while he screams I'm so and so.

When he tears off the blindfold, he's standing on the sunshine road of his hometown.

B 00007（身份不明）

电线杆下的长舌妇忽然沉默，
地下火焰的耳朵正在将她的话语捕捉。
地下刮胡子的男人刮得满脸是血。
我们中间消逝的人此刻正在地下跋涉。
我精神的探照灯照见地下那些秘密的、橘红的肉体，也照见我们
中间消逝的人：
他偶然攀上墙头，窥见无声的鲜花，而那鲜花的惊叫使他坠落。
他不知是否回到了童年，他不知这是死亡还是永生之所。
迷路在异乡，风雨在远方，迎面撞见昔日的债主，他一脸笑容掩
盖不住惊慌失措。
但是共同的饥饿使他们拥抱，但是共同的语言他们宁肯不说。
走过歌剧院，走过洗衣店，像两名暗探他们混进别人的晚宴，在
地下异乡他们找不到厕所。
三名警察将他们逮捕，十八名妇女控告他们龌龊。
他眼看昔日的债主出示伪造的通行证，而他只能掏出一小盒清凉
油。
"请收下这微薄的礼物"，他说。但是牢房已经备好。他被蒙上
眼睛推进牢房，他大喊大叫我是某某。
等他摘下眼罩他却怒气全消：他站在故乡的阳光大道。

C 00024

A lotus flower floats in the sky, bird shit is caught by the earth, a fist punches through his ear. On the sunshine road he runs naked.

The fire in the sky is extinguished. Dust from earth counts for how man lives? He hears his nickname echo, a child walks into his heart.

At dawn, a chair appears in the village of his heart.

In the heart, a chess game starts.

Nine surrenders, ten rebellions, three executions, four killings.

Moonlight shines on the polluted river, dew cleanses the romantic ghosts.

At the Carnival Festival, ghosts step on his heels, the beginning of misfortune: a thick-browed man pushes him out of the line.

Years later he lights his first match.

"Let it be," he whispers to a butterfly.

On the road cleaned by butterflies, on the road that used to be fields, every home looks like one he rebelled against, every magpie falls.

The old world crumbles around his feet, his body becomes transparent.

Sorrow fills his temples like the Big Dipper fills the roof...dizzy with coughing, he forgets the script of life.

C 00024

有一朵荷花在天空飘浮。有一滴鸟粪被大地接住。有一只拳头穿
进他的耳孔。在阳光大道他就将透明。

天空的大火业已熄灭，地上的尘土是多少条性命？他听见他的乳
名被呼喊，一个孩子一直走进他的心中。

他心中的黎明城寨里只有一把椅子。

他心中的血腥战场上摆开了棋局。

他历经九次屈从、十次反抗、三次被杀、四次杀人。

月光洒落在污秽的河面，露水洗干净浪漫的鬼魂。

在狂欢节上，鬼魂踩掉他的鞋跟。厄运开始，他被浓眉大眼的家
伙推出队列。

多年以后他擦亮第一根火柴。"就这样吧"，他对一只蝴蝶小声
耳语。

在蝴蝶清扫的道路两旁，在曾经是田埂的道路两旁，每一个院落
都好像他当年背叛的家庭，每一只喜鹊都在堕落。

旧世界被拆除到他的脚边，他感觉自身开始透明。

忧伤涌上他的太阳穴，就像屋顶上涌出七星北斗。……一阵咳嗽，
一阵头晕，让他把人生的台词忘得一干二净。

D 00059

He was King of Chu, who razed Wo Fang Palace.

He was Black Tornado, who tore the emperor's pardon to pieces.

With the heart of a king, he sits between liquor bottles and birdcages. Peasant-faced, his sons and grandsons sing pop tunes. They vacation in the country.

After the night, fog, after thunder, his brain leaks. He speaks different tongues in different rooms. His last territory is his house.

He was once Emperor Li. His poetry negated the crime of losing his nation.

He was once Emperor Hui of the Sung who allowed peacocks to stroll in his court.

Too feeble to talk about his past—famines, harvests, beggars' justice, gamblers' legends, too weak to talk, he hiccups at spring.

At dusk he walks streets drunkenly. He curses himself, but people think he's cursing this paradise. His poor, embarrassed father waits at the dead end, ready to box him in the ear.

D 00059

他曾经是楚霸王，一把火烧掉阿房宫。

他曾经是黑旋风，撕烂朝廷的招安令。

而现在他坐在酒瓶和鸟笼之间，内心接近地主的晚年。他的儿子们长着农业的面孔，他的孙子们唱着流行歌曲去乡村旅行。

经过黑夜、雾霭、雷鸣电闪，他的大脑进了水。他在不同的房间里说同样的话。他最后的领地仅限于家庭。

他曾经是李后主，用诗歌平衡他亡国的恶名。

他曾经是宋徽宗，允许孔雀进入他的大客厅。

但他无力述说他的过去：那欠收、那丰收，那乞丐中的道义、那赌徒中的传说。他无力述说他的过去，一到春天就开始打嗝。

无数个傍晚他酒气熏天穿街过巷。他谩骂自己，别人以为他在谩骂这时代的天堂。他贫苦的父亲、羞惭的父亲等在死胡同里，准

He used to be a son.

Once a father, he now plays with a pair of walnuts.

His life, full of wrong words, is an unpublishable memoir; his heart is white terror waiting for nonsense.

He wakes the caged birds with chirping. He leaves home without keys, an empty bottle in his hand.

E 00183

Confucius said: "At thirty, a man stands."

At thirty, the doctor diagnosed his infertility. His clan will vanish. He shattered china, burnt books, wailed himself to sleep.

Confucius said: "At forty, a man is no longer puzzled."

At forty, he trembled at the sound of singing, guilt made him give up his golden Buddha. He moved out of his mansion, turned over a new leaf. A weak man wants nothing but peace.

Confucius said: "At fifty, a man knows the mandate of heaven."

Porridge stains all over his fifty-year-old wife, he brings her vegetables and a small sea bass after school. Late blooming love is like the rusty oil in a wok.

备迎面给他一记耳光。

他曾经是儿子，现在是父亲；

他曾经是父亲，现在玩着一对老核桃。

充满错别字的一生像一部无法发表的回忆录；他心中有大片空白
像白色恐怖需要胡编乱造来填补。

当他笼中的小鸟进入梦乡，他学着鸟叫把它们吵醒。他最后一次
拎着空酒瓶走出家门，却忘了把钥匙带上。

E 00183

子曰："三十而立。"

三十岁，他被医生宣判没有生育能力。这预示着他庞大的家族不
能再延续。他砸烂瓷器，他烧毁书籍，他抱头痛哭，然后睡去。

子曰："四十而不惑。"

四十岁，笙歌震得他浑身发抖，强烈的犯罪感使他把祖传的金佛
交还给人民。他迁出豪宅，洗心革面：软弱的人多么渴求安宁。

子曰："五十而知天命。"

五十岁的妻子浑身粥渍。从他任教的小学校归来，他给妻子带回
了瓜子菜、回回菜和一尾小黄鱼。迟到的爱情像铁锅里的油腥。

Confucius said: "At sixty, a man's ears are an obedient organ for Truth."

He lost his hearing at sixty: a loud world was reduced to expressions. He stared out of his window as if expecting a friend from far away to come share tea.

Confucius said: "At seventy, man does as he pleases without crossing the line."

In a moldy room, love is written on his heart. His last tooth awakens pain, teardrops run into his mouth.

"How Mount Tai is crumbling! How the beams rot! How withered the sage!" Confucius died at seventy-three, an immortal age.

He spreads paper, grinds ink, dips his brush. Every attempt to praise life has failed.

子曰："六十而耳顺。"

而他彻底失聪在他耳顺的年头：一个闹哄哄的世界只剩下奇怪的表情。他长时间呆望窗外，好像有人将不远万里来将他造访，来喝他的茶，来和他一起呆望窗外。

子曰："七十而从心所欲，不逾矩。"

在发霉的房间里，他七十岁的心灵爱上了写诗。最后一颗牙齿提醒他疼痛的感觉。最后两滴泪水流进他的嘴里。

"泰山其颓乎！梁木其坏乎！哲人其萎乎！"孔子死时七十有三，而他活到了死不了的年龄。

他铺纸，研墨，蘸好毛笔。但他每一次企图赞美生活都是白费力气。

F 00202 (identity unclear)

Laughter: someone is in his room. His first thought: dirty trick! The second: crime!

The door won't open. He shouts: "Get out!" But it sounds like begging: he has sung too many decadent songs.

To be shut out of one's home is like crashing into a radio; he can hear drinking games inside.

Now, the street is crowded with tailors and nannies, all advising him to "swallow." But he shoves a finger down his throat, orders the guy in his stomach leave.

Vomit clears the mind. A dead rat scuttles at his feet. He catches the happy crowd in a garden, but they shout: "Get out!"

Someone else's clouds float in the sky, his face is covered with paint. At the city gate he hands a handkerchief to the shepherd who ate his last sheep.

He goes home, the laughter is still there. He shouts: "Get out!" but it bounces back.

"Get out—get out—get out." Repeat this three times, it'll sound like a poem.

F 00202（身份不明）

别人的笑声：别人在他的房间里。他脑海中闪现第一个词：勾当！
他脑海中闪现第二个词：罪行！
他用力推门，但门推不开。他拼命高喊："滚出去！"但他分明
是在乞求：他唱过太多的靡靡之音。
进不了自家的门，好像进不了说话的收音机：好像每一件事物都
在播音，他甚至听到肚子里有人在行酒令。
来了满街的裁缝，来了满街的保姆，他们劝他"忍着点儿"。但
他硬是把手指抠进咽喉，命令肚子里的家伙："滚出去！"
一阵呕吐让他清爽，一只死耗子让他绕行。他追上快乐的人群，
进入百花盛开的园圃。他听到众人喝斥："滚出去！"
（哦，谁能代替他滚出去，他就代替谁去死。）
天空飘满别人的云朵，他脸上挂着别人的石灰。城门洞里牧羊人
吃光了自己的羊群，他递上手绢让他擦嘴。
他再次回到自家的门口，听见房间里的笑声依旧不息。他再次高
喊："滚出去！"回答他的也是"滚出去！"
"滚出去——滚出去——滚出去——"这声音重复三遍以后听起
来就像一首诗。

His ears are used to elegant words. He'd rather cut them off than listen to the moan of mankind. Turned on by a porno he accidentally opened, he began to praise marriage vehemently.

Still, he dreams of a female stranger spreading her legs to reveal her peach petals. He wakes believing he's met the ideal one.

He never learned to piss on the streets in elementary school, never learned to hide his diary in middle school. He learned from history that gazing at plums could quench thirst, learned how to adjust the seasons with the wind of his soul.

When he can't take it any more, he ends his life—drops dead at meetings or on a square. His illness appears at his beck, a great weapon that allows him to live with conscience. The body, hidden under the ocean of life, comes up occasionally for air.

It's raining over the world. Every crook is posing for a picture.

In his late years, magpies sang for weeks on his porch. He inherited the estate of his long lost uncle. It allowed him to seek his edification alone, repeatedly made him check the locks on the windows and doors.

At sixty, he studied classical medicine.

At seventy, he showed interest in spirit and eternity.

G 00319

让他那习惯于优雅问候的耳朵去倾听人类的呻吟还不如将他的耳
朵割去。他碰巧打开的一本色情画报刺激他强烈地赞美一夫一妻。
可有时在梦中也会有陌生女人叉开两腿向他暴露那春天的桃花一
朵，于是醒来他焦灼地要求自己相信他是遇见了"理想"的化身。
他小学不曾学会随地小便，他中学不曾学会藏起日记。他从历史
中学会了望梅止渴，他用心灵之风来调节四季。

当他难过到极点他就让生命中断，他就倒在会场上、广场上或办
公室里。他以招之即来的疾病作武器赢得一生无愧于良心。他以
父母所给的躯体小心潜泳于生活的汪洋只偶尔到水面换口气。

全世界都在下雨，全世界的阴谋家都摆好了照相的姿势。

晚年，喜鹊落在他的阳台上歌唱了一星期。他久无音讯的叔父变
成一笔丰厚的遗产渡海穿山找到他家里。这足够他在苍蝇的嗡嗡
声中独善其身，这迫使他反复察看门窗是否关紧。

六十岁，他开始研读各民族的医药经典。

七十岁，他关心永恒和灵魂诸问题。

H 00325

A part time intellectual, he depends on social order, but his soul disagrees.

If he dies, there'll be chaos in the country and his soul will fill with questions.

As the boss, only his soul knows his cowardice.

He leaves teeth marks of administration on the apple, signs a worm-like name on documents. But his soul is more into games.

Locked into investments, his anxious soul paces in circles.

He's amazed by the water pipe's flowing beauty. Too much makes him impotent, yet his soul jumps on.

He disguises his heartbeat when his rival tries to strip him naked— friendship is built between the two enemies.

He learns emotion through loss and gain, leads the masses in singing for tomorrow, yet his soul longs for the past.

H 00325

生为半个读书人他依赖于既定的社会秩序，而他的灵魂不同意。

他若突然死亡，一群人中间就会混乱迭出，对此他的灵魂恰好充满好奇。

在一群人中间他说了算，而他的灵魂了解他的懦弱。

他在苹果上咬出行政的牙印，他在文件上签署蚯蚓的连笔字，而他的灵魂对于游戏更关心。

在利益的大厦里他闭门不出，他的灵魂急躁得来回打转。

水管里流出的小美人儿让他发愣，太美的人儿使他阳萎，而他的灵魂扑上去。

他必须小心掩饰自己的心跳，他的敌人要将他彻底揭穿，而在两者的灵魂之间建立起友谊。

他从权衡利弊中学会了抒情，他率领众人歌颂美好的明天，而他的灵魂只想回到往昔。

It's impossible for him to return to the riverboat at 9:00 pm, return to the mountain path at 6:00.

A ringing phone ruins his afternoon good mood. He puts the receiver down, gazes at the mountain range at sunset, a flash of animals startle him into a cold sweat.

In his soul sharp teeth are growing.

I 00326

He should have been born in the 19th century. His elegant handwriting would have attracted nature lovers.

If born in Russia, he would be waiting for the "ice maiden" in Pushkin's garden.

But he watched wrinkled clouds, white liquid dripping from broken glass. A tiny black figure kicked and punched in his brain.

When city kids moved to 14th century villages, his whistling father lured him to the of 21st to drive out the old century's ill star.

Thoughts spread through his limbs, thoughts like pigeons jumping into the fire. On a full-moon night, he screamed himself hoarse.

回到夜晚九点的江上扁舟,回到清晨六点的山中小径,而他不能这样做。

一阵急促的电话铃毁了他一个下午的好心情。他放下电话,眺望日落处绵亘的群山,一群他猛然想到的野兽惊得他冒出一身冷汗,而他的灵魂正在长出锋利的犬齿。

I 00326

他本应该出生在 19 世纪,他娟媚的字迹不会缺少游山玩水的知音。
他本应该出生在俄国,本应该在普希金的花园中静候冰雪的少女。
但是生活叫他心慌意乱:他看到起皱的云团,他看到扯断的草茎上流下乳白色的液体。一个小黑人儿在他脑子里拳打脚踢。
当大多数城市里的孩子吹着口哨落户 14 世纪的乡村,他的父亲把他引上 21 世纪的锦绣阶梯,而他多想赶走 20 世纪的灾难之星。
思想在肢体里蔓延,思想的鸽子卷入火把的骚乱。他在一个满月的夜晚喊哑了嗓子。

History congealed into a court sentence. He should have died in 1976, but death caught the bullet. He stood too quickly from the latrine pit and saw the stars of freedom.

Escaped from death. Pear blossoms in autumn. Pushkin grins in the mirror.

Now, he only drinks the best wine, rides the wildest girls. He flies against the wind of time, watching black sheep concert in the grassland.

He should have sung like a wind chime, but he kept silent as a kite.

He should have been beaten blue and black like the poor, but he became the master of clouds like XO.

历史，人生，凝缩为一纸判决。他本应该死在 1976 年，但死神
接住了射向他的子弹。
他好像从茅坑上一下子站起，眼前闪烁着自由的金星。
大难不死。梨树在秋天开花。普希金在镜中怪笑。
从此他饮最醇的酒，从此他骑最野的姑娘。他逆着时代的风向起
飞，俯身看到黑压压的羊群在旷野上举行一场怀旧的音乐会。
他本应该像风铃一样歌唱，可是他像风筝一样沉默。
他本应该像穷人一样在乌云上磕得鼻青脸肿，可是他像 XO 马爹
利一样成了白云的主人。

J 00568 (identity not clear)

A paper man, soaked blue in ink.

A paper man, dizzy in dawn light.

He has a shadow, a name. Determined to do something big, he learns to bend and yawn.

He seeks the sensation of his soul fleeing: like paper falling from the sky.

Curious, he lights a fire and burns off an arm.

He controls his fate with his other hand.

Doctrines and habits block him, crowds crush him. He tries to raise his sage's whip, but time raises its bottom to his face.

He shines his shoes after the first girl brought flowers. But at night, he panicks at the static in his shirt.

He rushes to hide in books, falls into the trashcan where he lectures his fear into a challenge.

Fighting the bodies of flesh and blood, he builds a papier-mâché rocking chair.

He mimics human voice, mimics their ambitions.

J 00568（身份不明）

一个纸人，在墨水里泡蓝。

一个纸人，在晨光中晕眩。

他有了影子，有了名字，决心大干一场。他学会了弯腰和打哈欠。

他寻找灵魂出窍的感觉："那也许就像纸片在空中飞落。"

他好奇地点燃一堆火，一下子烧掉一只胳膊。

他必须善于自我保护，他必须用另一只手将命运把握。

教条和习俗拦住他，懒散的人群要将他挤瘪。

他试着挥起先知的皮鞭，时代就把屁股撅到他面前。

在第一个姑娘向他献花之后他擦亮皮鞋。但是每天夜里，衬衫磨擦出的静电火花都叫他慌乱。

他慌乱地躲进书页，他慌乱地掉进纸篓；他在纸篓中高谈阔论，他把慌乱转变为挑战。

挑战那些血肉之躯，用纸张糊一把纸人的安乐椅。

他模仿人类的声音，他模仿人类的雄心。

如果你用针来刺他的手指，他不会流血；如果你打击他，实际上打击的却是别人。

Prick his fingertip, he won't bleed; hit him, you're hitting someone else.

K 01704

Humbleness is the only virtue that won't win love.

Endurance turned him into an abandoned building.

He shut his mouth to avoid political torture. He protected freedom for love in the red capital.

He watched dull women lounge and great women elevate men.

But the great are like phantoms. He climbed the steps, knocking hesitantly. A little girl opened the door and said, "Wrong place."

Stumbling between two families, the seasons diminished, only his lustful fantasy shimmered in the rain. A lonely playboy swung in hell.

The tea got cold, the old photo album disappeared. His heart murmured, his dreams pushed to the finale. He died next to his wife: his corpse is our Old Meng.

He turned into a hunched ghost, refusing to hand over his love's black box.

K 01704

谦卑是唯一一种不能赢得爱情的美德。
忍耐最终把自己变成一幢无人居住的大厦。
比如这个人，把沉默闭在嘴里，避开政治的刑罚。数十个年头，
在红色首都，为了爱一个女人他需要自由。
他看到无聊的女性在身边走动，而那伟大的女性引领别人上升。
伟大的女性如同幻影。他攀上幻影的楼梯，他犹豫再三去造访那
幻影一家人，开门的小姑娘说："你敲错了门。"
踟蹰在两个家庭之间，四季的风景越来越平淡，只有风雨中淫荡
的幻想越来越灿烂。一个孤独的公子哥荡起地狱里的秋千。
杯中的茶水凉了，旧相像册不翼而飞。他的心脏发出怪声，他的
梦境推向剧终。他死在妻子的身边：一具尸体那是我们的老孟。
他化作一个佝偻的幻影，至死没有交出爱情的黑匣子。
现在他已可以飘入那伟大女性的高楼上的窗口。这就是老一代的
风流韵事，只有傻瓜才为之心痛。

He floated into the window where the great woman lived. This is the love story of the old generation. Only fools feel pain for him.

L 01933

...

M 02345

In his memory every saint is handsome. He left the crowd, shameful of his ugliness and walked into his grave.

He woke at midnight with a start, turned on all the lights but nothing there belonged in his home.

Who's the master of this world? Whose body is he using? His life is over, his soul in debt decides:

A book worm, not humble enough for eagles, nor prejudiced enough to flaunt. He asked flowers what made them so angry, their bright blossoms predicted his misfortune.

His wife, born from an intellectual's family, died beneath thugs' sticks.

When he returned from exile, he saw his second wife bathing. He could not live on because he still remembered.

L 01933

…………

M 02345

他印象中的贤哲无不眉宇英俊，而他容貌粗糙，怎能跻身其间？
他惭愧地离开人群步入荒野，不期然来到自己的坟前。

惊醒在夜半的人打开所有的灯盏，可灯光所照亮的并非他的家园。
谁是这世界的主人？他使用着谁的躯体？欠账的一生大限将至，
他用欠账的灵魂做出判断：一个书呆子，既无足够的灵巧以向鹰
隼表示谦恭，亦无足够的偏见以向鹰屎表示傲慢。他问鲜花被什
么所激怒，怒放到极致的鲜花给了他不祥的预感。

当国家贫穷到只剩下争斗，他那出身于书香门第的妻子死于暴徒
的乱棍之下。

从穷山恶水的流放地归来，他的第二个妻子在洗澡。但他已无法
生活因为他思想；他时时孤单因为他怀念。

万物的阴影横卧大地，一团乌云涌进他的嘴里化作一口浓痰，他
不知该吐出去还是不该吐出去。月光意味着遗忘，清风意味着仁
慈，身边打呼噜的女人意味着历史在继续。

而他的意志被剥夺，却不知剥夺其意志的究竟是何人。

Shadows lay on the ground, clouds poured into his mouth. Moonlight meant forgetting, a breeze meant kindness. The snoring woman next to him meant history went on.

His will was robbed, but by whom and why, he had no idea.

N 05180 (Identity unclear)

Small is beautiful, small is clean, small is safe.

Small like an egg, like a button, even smaller, smaller, like an insect in amber.

His sweat-stained hand towel, his footprints on the grass. It's not that he couldn't produce garbage, he just didn't want to become it; he shrank to reach that goal.

Dust covered his face, he shrank.

On the road, he remembered a joke; laughing, he shrank.

Children gathered sunshine with a magnifying glass. He dodged the light. but still, his skin smoldered.

He lost his way, couldn't recognize what was what. He climbed on the train's engine, luckily it didn't move.

N 05180（身份不明）

小的是美的，小的是干净的，小的是安全的。

像鸡蛋一样小的，像纽扣一样小，更小，更小，最好像昆虫一样厝身于透明的琥珀里。

毛巾上滞留着他的汗渍，草叶上滞留着他的脚印。他并非不能制造垃圾，只是不想让自己成为垃圾；他通过缩小自己来达到目的。

尘土扑了他一满脸，他缩小一下。

走在路上，想起一个笑话，他哈哈大笑，他缩小一下。

孩子们用放大镜聚集太阳的光芒，他一闪身躲过那滚烫的焦点。但他的身上还是冒起了青烟。

他已不辨方向，他已不辨物体。他爬上火车的额头，幸好那冒失鬼一动未动。

世界之大全在于他身子之小。他愈贴近大地，便愈害怕天空。他冒险抓住生锈的弹簧，他心满意足地在落叶下躲雨。

没有朋友，没有敌人，他一小口一小口地吃着孤独的蛋糕。

没有任何禁区他不能进入，没有任何秘密他不能分享。但太小的他甚至无法爱上一个姑娘，甚至无法惹出最小的麻烦。

The world depended on the smallness of his body. The closer he pressed into the earth, the more he feared the sky. He grabbed the rusty spring, happily listened to rain under the fallen leaves.

No friend, no enemy, he tasted the cake gingerly.

No secret or forbidden place could stop him. But he was too small to fall in love, too small to stir up troubles.

O 09734

He was born in the rivers and rice paddies. Wind of agriculture dried his bottom. He begged protection from temple gods.

He studied until midnight when female ghosts appeared to wash his feet; he ploughed the fields until they were barren.

Venus shined in the sky, his boat sailed beneath. With the pleasure of eloping, he knocked open Nero's door, but when they strolled in the grand square, his bad breath offended Nero.

Gods listened to his babbling, fools fed him crumbs. He was a success in his hometown: when he returned he became a dictator.

He locked his drawers.

He held poison in his mouth.

O 09734

他出生的省份遍布纵横的河道、碧绿的稻田。农业之风吹凉了他
的屁股。他请求庙里的神仙对他多加照看。

他努力学习，学习到半夜女鬼为他洗脚；他努力劳动，劳动到地
里不再有收成。

长庚星闪耀在天边，他的顺风船开到了长庚星下面。带着私奔的
快感他敲开尼禄的家门，但漫步在雄伟的广场，他的口臭让尼禄
感到厌烦。

另一个半球的神祇听见他的蠢话，另一个半球的蠢人招待他面包
渣。可在故乡人看来他已经成功：一回到祖国他就在有限的范围
里实行起小小的暴政。

他给一个个抽屉上了锁。

他在嘴里含着一口有毒的血。

他想象所有的姑娘顺从他的蹂躏。

他把一张支票签发给黑夜。

转折的时代，小人们酒足饭饱。他松开皮带，以小恩小惠换得喝彩。

在一个冬天的早晨他横尸于他的乡间别墅，有人说是谋杀，有人
说是自裁。

He fantasized about raping all the girls on earth.

He wrote a check to darkness.

In the time of change, small people had enough to eat and drink. He unbuckled his belt and won cheers with small favors.

On a winter morning he died in his country house. Someone said it was a murder, others said it was suicide.

P 09772

Childhood of calcium deficiency. Youth of iron deficiency. There was no moonlight in his memory. No next life in sleep.

Strange sounds filled nature, his hearing dulled.

He sighed, got angry, dragged the mop through the dark hallway. Anxiety bit his middle years. He only smiled to restore his energy.

His smoke-stained fingers withered flowers. He watered the weeds but angered the earth. It shook, cracked. Trees rolled to him in mad waves. He escaped the collapsing city! He cried till stars toppled.

The statue of fire and picture of water didn't give him the third eye; his stolen happiness prevented greater disasters.

P 09772

缺钙的童年。缺铁的青春。记忆中没有月光。睡梦中没有来世。
大自然奇怪的声响已经够多，只是他的听觉趋向于迟钝。
他叹气，他发怒，他拖着墩布穿过不见天日的走廊。无名的烦躁
齿咬着他人生的中年，仅仅为了恢复体力他才露出笑脸。
他那被烟草熏黄的手指养不活花朵。他给野草浇水不曾想又把大
地惹火。大地颤动，开裂，树木卷起疯狂的巨浪朝他涌来。他逃
出倒塌中的城市！哭得星星坠落。
但是火的雕像、水的图画并末赋予他第三只眼；他被阻止的幸福
阻止了他蒙受更大的苦难。
他像猪一样等待被宰杀，他像涂鸦一样等待被抹去，他像橘子汁
一样等待被啜饮。
他神态无辜好像世界在犯罪。他长出男人的乳房，把世界变成一
个色鬼。
不做噩梦，不看太阳，不争善恶，不作打算。
他一边咒骂着米饭中的老鼠屎，一边把自己吃得大腹便便。

He waited for slaughter like a pig, waited to be erased, to be drunk like orange juice.

He looked innocent as if he were master of the world's sins. He grew breasts, made the world addicted to sex.

He didn't have nightmares, didn't look at the sun, didn't fight for right or wrong, didn't calculate.

Cursing the mouse droppings in his rice, he stuffed himself obese.

Q 10014

...

R 10897 (identity unclear)

...

Q 10014

....

R 10897（身份不明）

....

S 12121

图书馆好似巨大的心房。图书馆里有大洋深处的寂静。但他听到一个女人的哭声，但他始终未找到这哭泣的女人。

他从书架上抽出的每一本书都已被涂抹得难以辨认。他想找寻问题的答案，却发现问题已从疑问句被调整为陈述句。

S 12121

The library is a giant heart. Inside, it is as quiet as the ocean's bottom. He hears an invisible woman weeping.

Every book he pulls from the shelf is scribbled on. He tries to find the answers, but discovers they've gone down the drain.

The creation days are over, what's left is emptiness. Everything he wants to say has been said; everything he wants to do is poured in the rain.

"Two negatives don't always make a positive, like a blind man wearing mask remains blind..." As soon as he wrote this, a man with sunglasses accused him of plagiarism.

He stole words from a non-exist saint, eyes red and swollen.

He doubts his existence: has his life been canceled?

He gives his seat to spiders. He soaks his head in cold water. Of those he can hear, see or touch, how many belong to him? What fit in his imagination?

He writes: "Night gives birth to a little bird, which is all other birds; it sings in eighteen ways, but it's still just a singing bird."

He writes: "No matter how beautiful, how kind, brave and blessed, no matter how we praise the sacred beast, qi lin doesn't exist."

Gradually he understands: he must sue to honor his canceled life.

创造的日子早已完结，留给他的只有空虚一片。他想说出的一切别人都已说出；他想做的一切无异于向雨中泼水。

"否定之否定并不一定是肯定，就像一个蒙面的瞎子还是瞎子……"他在纸上一写出这句话，就有一个戴墨镜的家伙指责他抄袭。

他抄袭了不存在的先哲，他两眼红肿。

他怀疑自己的存在：他的生命是否已被事先取消？

他把座位让给蜘蛛。他把头浸在凉水里。那些可以被听的，可以被看的，可以被触摸的，有多少属于他自己；什么东西，既符合他的想象，又符合他的推理？

他写道："黑夜里诞生了一只小鸟，与别的小鸟并无二致；用十八种方法歌唱，无非是鸟叫而已。"

他写道："无论被描述得多么美丽，多么仁义，多么勇武，多么圣洁，麒麟是不存在的。"

他渐渐明白了自己的使命：用他那已被事先取消的生命打一场有关名誉的官司。

T 18060

The hidden water drops. The hidden lips. The hidden castle in the air. The hidden Monday.

After Homer, after Milton, he wants to see everything with his blind eyes, he wants to walk down stairs with his withered legs.

He turns at the sound of tearing paper. At the sound of wiping glass he comes out. He calls the man's name.

It is fall and his friends leave. Autumn wind blows at him alone.

He dreams: all the heroes in heaven leave their resumes on earth. Whoever he dreams, he resurrects.

He sees another reality: fire and sorrow, sunlight and road. He joins history and rejects the landscape.

He rejects the gray and mad knocking on the door. In the world of a blind man, he is allowed to see.

He knocks over water buckets, bumps into walls, every step is a possible end, but long ago, he turned himself into an abyss overflowing with creamy paths and brightly-lit banquets.

T 18060

被遮蔽的水滴。被遮蔽的嘴唇。被遮蔽的空中楼阁。被遮蔽的星期一。

在荷马之后，在弥尔顿之后，他要用他瞎掉的双眼看到这一切，他要用他无力的双脚走下楼梯。

背后传来撕纸的声音，他转过脸来。背后传来擦玻璃的声音，他准确叫出那人的姓名。

这是秋天。友人们带走了他们的时代，秋风便集中吹向他一人。

而他的梦境在扩大：满天空的英灵只在人间留下一段段简历。他梦见谁，谁就再活一次。

他以同情看到另一种真实：火焰与悲哀、霞光与大道。他加入历史的行列，意味着拒绝身边的风景；

意味着拒绝他眼前的灰暗以及灰暗中狂乱的砸门声。在一个盲人的世界上，他被允许看到另一种真实。

他踢到水桶，他撞着墙壁，他的每一步都有可能迈进深渊，但他早已把自己变成另一座深渊，容纳乳白色的小径和灯火通明的宴会厅。

The land that holds him, the land that holds his ancestors, his relatives, his friends, needs his birth as much as his death. He has little time to become himself.

The sound of herbs sizzling reminds him of how fragile humanity is. Only a blind man can see a blind man's smile.

U 20000

He forgives the crows of the countryside's roosters, forgives dusk as they sing. He forgives the stone grinder and B.C.'s casting technology.

He forgives the dry pen, the stubborn donkey. He forgives the female teacher in middle school, forgives this dumb woman for locking him in a dark classroom.

But he won't forgive the human folly, even though he forgives the sealed walls, the crowded streets, the flies, even the person with goose bumps in a warm room.

He forgives the crows' plummet, the chattering of flamingoes. But he won't forgive the rain of stones, the rain of tiles. Even though he has overcome his hot-temper.

He forgives the surrendering army, the judges who drink milk, his files, memos, decisions, but he won't forgive slogans, documents, books, and the typos in instructions.

这片承载他的土地，这片承载他的祖先、他的亲人、他的友人的土地，需要他诞生正如需要他死亡。他只有短暂的时间成为他自己。煎药的声音提醒他人性的脆弱。一个盲人的微笑只有盲人能够看清。

U 20000

他原谅乡村的鸡鸣、鸡鸣时分尚未消退的黑暗。他原谅原始的石磨、建筑中自秦代以来再无改进的筑板技术。他甚至怀念这一切。他原谅不出水的钢笔、不开窍的毛驴。他原谅惩罚学生的中学女教师，原谅这个头脑空虚的女人把他关进一间漆黑的教室。

但他不原谅人类的愚行，尽管他原谅封闭的院墙、拥挤的街道、飞行的苍蝇，尽管他原谅那个在温暖的房间里起鸡皮疙瘩的人。

他原谅乌鸦的俯冲、火烈鸟的饶舌。但他不原谅从天而降的石头之雨、瓦片之雨。尽管他早已克服了暴躁的脾气。

他原谅躺倒在地的军队、喝牛奶的法官，有关他的档案、传言、决定，但他不原谅标语、文件、书本、说明书中的错别字。

He forgives his children and wife for their betrayal; his weeping has never seen any words. Only today did we realize he had every reason to smash the radio.

But he didn't. He forgives belief in electricity, belief in water. How sad the shiny river! But he won't forgive the unbelieving sky. Where is he going? Who will he meet?

He forgives his cancer, his miserable funeral. He forgives the way he'd forgive rotten food. But he won't forgive the paper money they offered.

Twenty years after he died, we acknowledge him as a person.

Translated by by Wang Ping & Alex Lemon

他原谅背叛他的儿女、与他告别的妻子；他的哭泣从未见诸任何
文字。今天我们才知道他有充分理由砸烂他唯一值钱的收音机。
但他没有那样做。他原谅电的信仰、水的信仰，闪光的河流多么
忧郁！但他不原谅没有信仰的天空。他将何往？他将遇到什么人？
他原谅他的癌症、他的糟糕的葬礼以及出现在他葬礼上的乌云，
像原谅变质的饭菜。但他不原谅为他而焚化的纸钱。
在他死后二十年，我们追认他为一个人。

1995.11—1996.12

致谢　　　本诗选里的诗是由 Lucas Klein, Maghiel van Crevel, Sarah Anais Aubry，Tony Barnstone，Inara Cedrins, Michael Day, Brian Holton, John Keley, Lucas Klein, Robert Neather, George O'Connell, Pascale Petit, Wang Ping, Arthur Sze 等著名翻译家译成英文，谨致谢忱！

译者简介　　　Sarah Anais Aubry，中国文学研究者，曾为香港城市大学学生。

Tony Barnstone，美国诗人，曾获多种诗歌奖项。1980 年代曾与其父、诗人 Willis Barnstone 在北京居住。此外他还曾生活于肯尼亚和希腊，现居加利福尼亚，系 Whittier College 教授。编有 *Out of the Howling Storm: The New Chinese Poetry*（Wesleyan University Press）等多部与中国古今文学有关的书。

Inara Cedrins（岳流萤），美国诗人，出版有诗集 *Fugitive Connections*（2006）。曾作为语言教师短期任教于清华大学。

Maghiel van Crevel（柯雷），荷兰汉学家，莱顿大学教授，荷兰皇家学院院士。长期追踪中国当代诗歌的发展，著有 *Chinese Poetry in Times of Mind, Mayhem and Money*（Brill，2008；有中译本）。他用英语翻译的西川作品曾发表于香港中文大学 *Renditions*（《译丛》）、美国 Seneca Review（《西涅卡评论》）等杂志，并被收入由 Joseph S. M. Lau 与 Howard Goldblatt（葛浩文）编辑的 *The Columbia Anthology of Modern Chinese Literature*（《哥伦比亚版现代中国文选》）。

Michael Day（戴迈河），加拿大汉学家，荷兰莱顿大学文学博士，译有中国 1980 年代大量诗歌作品，但多数未出版。

Brian Holton（霍布恩），英国汉学家，《水浒传》苏格兰文本译者及杨炼诗集的主要英译者。他与杨炼、W.N. Herbert、秦晓宇等编辑出版过中国当代诗选 *Jade Ladder*（Bloodaxe，2012）。

John Keley（蒋凯利），英国汉学家，现执教于美国布朗大学，从事智能写作研究。

Lucas Klein（柯夏智），美国汉学家、耶鲁大学博士，西川诗歌在英语世界的主要译者。现执教于亚利桑那州立大学。在纽约 New Directions（新方向）出版社出版有两部西川英译诗集：*Notes on the Mosquito: Xi Chuan /Selected Poems*（2012）和 *Bloom and Other Poems*（2022）。前者获美国文学翻译家协会（ALTA）2013 Lucien Stryk Asian Translation Prize，并入围美国 2013 Best Translated Book Award；后者获 *The New York Times*（《纽约时报》）推荐。柯夏智也是北岛、多多、芒克的译者。

Robert Neather（倪若诚），英国汉学家，香港浸会大学翻译系主任、教授。Luby Chow 系其浸会大学学生。

George O'Connell，美国诗人，与 Diana Shi（史春波）长期居住于中国香港。两人合作翻译有不少中国当代诗歌作品。曾在 2008 年编辑美国 *Atlanta Review*（《亚特兰大评论》春夏合刊）中国当代诗歌专号。

Weijia Pan（潘伟嘉），中国赴美青年诗人、翻译家。

Pascale Petit，英国诗人，出版有多部诗集，曾两次入围 T.S. 艾略特奖。2004 年英国诗歌图书协会选择她作为"新一代诗人"（Next Generation Poet）。

Wang Ping（王屏），中国旅美诗人和小说家，先后受教于北京大学和纽约大学。执教于明尼苏达州圣保罗 Macalester College。1993 和 1996 年有作品被收入 *The Best American Poetry*（《美国最佳诗选》）。编有 *New Generation: Poems from China Today*（Hanging Loose Press, 1999）。西川《厄运》组诗系其与学生 Alex Lemon 合译。

Arthur Sze（施家彰），第二代华裔美国诗人。任教于多所大学，为美国印第安艺术学院退休教授。出版有多部诗集。曾任新墨西哥州圣达菲桂冠诗人、美国诗人协会主席，2019 年获美国国家图书奖。出版有中国古今诗人的译诗集 *The Silk Dragon*（Copper Canyon Press）。

图书在版编目（CIP）数据

西川诗歌英译选：汉英对照 / 杨四平主编. -- 上
海：上海文化出版社，2023.6
（当代汉诗英译丛书）
ISBN 978-7-5535-2744-4

Ⅰ.①西… Ⅱ.①杨… Ⅲ.①诗集—中国—当代—汉、英 Ⅳ.
①I227

中国国家版本馆CIP数据核字(2023)第080778号

出 版 人：姜逸青
责任编辑：黄慧鸣　张　彦
装帧设计：王　伟

书　　　名：**西川诗歌英译选**
作　　　者：杨四平
出　　　版：上海世纪出版集团　上海文化出版社
地　　　址：上海市闵行区号景路159弄A座三楼 201101
发　　　行：上海文艺出版社发行中心
　　　　　　上海市闵行区号景路159弄A座二楼 201101 www.ewen.co
印　　　刷：苏州市越洋印刷有限公司
开　　　本：889×1194 1/32
印　　　张：7.125
印　　　次：2023年6月第一版 2023年6月第一次印刷
书　　　号：ISBN 978-7-5535-2744-4/I.1054
定　　　价：58.00元
告 读 者：如发现本书有质量问题请与印刷厂质量科联系 T：0512-68180628